BYLINES & DEADLINES

by

Kimberly Vinje

CCB Publishing
British Columbia, Canada

Bylines & Deadlines

Copyright ©2008 by Kimberly Vinje
ISBN-13   978-1-926585-00-0
First Edition

Library and Archives Canada Cataloguing in Publication

Vinje, Kimberly, 1970-
Bylines & deadlines / written by Kimberly Vinje.
ISBN 978-1-926585-00-0
I. Title. II. Title: Bylines and deadlines.
PS3622.I563B94 2008   813'.6   C2008-905706-6

United States Copyright Office Registration # TXu 1-579-438

Publisher: CCB Publishing
British Columbia, Canada
www.ccbpublishing.com

To Gary - you are my rock, and I love you.

Acknowledgements

So often a day passes when we forget to tell people how much they mean to us or how thankful we are to have them in our lives. Not only do I promise to try harder to show my appreciation every day, but I also want to say it here in case someday I'm not able.

Gary Tucker, it didn't seem right not to acknowledge you even though I dedicated this to you. You see the best in me. I don't know how you do it, but I'm really thankful you do! I love you.

To my parents Kathy & Jerry - you have given me so much and I don't think I'll ever be able to thank you enough. You are appreciated and loved very much! Greg & Gina Vinje - I love you. Jake, Ella and Will Vinje - you have no idea how much joy you've given me. I love you more than you can know!

My Gram, Ann Weber who would have gotten so much pride from her "little granddaughter" writing a book, and my grandpa, Giles Weber from whom I got my passion for writing - I know you're in Heaven cheering for me. I love and miss you both. To Shirley Crowe, Sverre Vinje and my extended family members, I love you all very much!

Thank you to my friends - especially Terri Konte, who challenged me to write this and Maria Hinkel, who drove me to pursue publishing it. I can't forget Carol Rock for pointing me in the right direction to get this published and Lisa Warndorf and Vicky Mayer, the "Eagle Eyes" who edited this book for me. I owe thanks to Tammy Quatman for helping me with the website and Nikki Hufford, Nancy Conly, Ruth Hitchcock, Maria Brennen, Linda Skilbeck, Ron Cosby, Michael Adee, Melinda Proffitt and Karen Schroer for their many years of unbelievable friendship. Everyone has been so supportive through this whole process - hey it only took 10 years! I love you for all the strength and encouragement you give me!

Cody, you are an amazing gift and so full of love. Thanks for letting me read portions of this to you so I could hear how the words sounded. More importantly, thanks for faking interest when you tilted your head from side to side while you listened. I love you.

To Paul Rabinovitch at CCB Publishing, thank you for your patience and encouragement!

There are so many others… I'll get you in the sequel!

Prologue

Kristine Larkin died at the age of 25 - just when she had begun to live her dream. She was an ambitious reporter, who worked hard to gain the respect of her editors and the people she approached when she had a good lead on a story. She was young and attractive - two strikes against her in the cut-throat fight for a byline. She ached to be taken seriously and grew more and more frustrated when she wasn't. She didn't hide that frustration well and commonly used sarcasm in her poor and unconscious self-defense strategy.

She knew rumors swirled when she was hired fresh out of a small town university by a paper as large and reputable as the New York Chronicle. That's why she was more tenacious, more aggressive and more arrogant than the seasoned reporters could accept from an unproven kid with a journalism degree. She was unexpected in their world.

After a year, some of the reporters started to recognize her talents, but most of them still didn't like her. The publisher and editors loved her. She raised the bar for some of the veterans who had become reactive and complacent. Instead of seeking a big story, a few of the reporters would wait for someone to drop one into their laps. They were living off their reputation. When Kristine arrived, she began to find the big stories on her own. She networked with anyone and everyone. She flirted with security guards, and she commiserated with administrative assistants.

Her subtle manipulation of people bordered on the brazen. She finessed people using two rules: 1) a man's vulnerabilities stemmed from ego and libido and 2) a woman's vulnerabilities resided in ego and maternal instinct. If she could find common ground, she could work a person into revealing what she wanted to know. She almost always had an ulterior motive for engaging someone on the personal level, which she justified by convincing herself the ends justified the means.

She spent so much energy making contacts outside the office she didn't show much interest in her co-workers. She spent her time away from work working. She would listen to police scanners, read old news stories written by journalists she admired, or she'd go to a bar where she knew people with potential stories and secrets would be drinking...and talking too much.

There was one exception to her disposable view of people - a man named Derrick. Derrick was a nurse at one of the busiest hospitals in the city. Privacy laws prevented patient information from being freely given by medical professionals, but Derrick liked to talk even if he wouldn't see his name in print. He seemed to get some pleasure from knowing he was "an unnamed source" or maybe it was sticking it to the establishment that drove him. Most likely it was that he liked knowing things others didn't and wasn't good at keeping secrets for strangers. Either way, what had started as a reporter luring someone into her network of sources had turned into the closest thing she had to a friendship. Derrick didn't give you the option to ignore him, and he was likable. So, Kristine allowed herself an occasional Sunday afternoon shopping or trying a new restaurant with him, but she always seemed to have one ear tuned to the conversation next to her. He was everything she wasn't - a free-spirit and more interested in his personal than his professional life. He had different priorities, and Kristine found him interesting, even if she didn't understand him.

On the rare occasion Kristine stopped chasing her next byline, she could be enjoyable. No one saw this side often enough to admit it existed, though. In fact, no one really knew too much about her - and really, she didn't either. Becoming a Pulitzer Prize winning journalist was her goal - okay, obsession - and the rest of her life could wait. Kristine had no idea how little time she had.

This is the story of the demise of Kristine Larkin.

Chapter One

It wasn't every day Kristine Larkin took time to notice something as inconsequential as a pretty sky. Today was different. The sun had just risen and the sky was so blue it reached out to touch you. Kristine had just come out of her favorite coffee shop with her vanilla flavored (and very expensive) coffee. The smell of the shop meant a new day, new opportunities and a new byline. She inhaled deeply and smiled to herself at the excitement of the possibilities of the story she would dig up today. She pulled her sunglasses down over her eyes and smoothed the hair where the glasses had been sitting. She stopped at a crosswalk and took a sip of coffee while she waited.

It was already hot. The air was so thick with humidity it stuck to your skin. Summer in New York. It was oppressive at best. It also smelled - really bad. Urine from the homeless or a drunk guy who thought it was a good idea to relieve himself on a sidewalk after a night of bar hopping baked into the concrete. Garbage cans along the street sped the deterioration of discarded food and acted as a beacon for rats and roaches from what she was sure were the depths of hell. When Kristine moved to New York, the rodents were the toughest part of her culture shock. Oh, and the sewers... the sewers were sewers. Enough said.

Kristine hiked her bag up on her shoulder and pushed her sunglasses up her nose. She flipped her long, thick brown ponytail over her tanned shoulder as the "walk" light flashed white, and she started across the street. She had gotten sun just from walking around town every day. The tan made her eyes seem even greener.

There weren't many New Yorkers up and about at this hour

so the streets were just busy and not jam packed. As she dodged people crossing the street against her, someone slammed into her so hard her coffee splashed through the little hole in the white cap. She jumped back to avoid being splattered with coffee.

"Hey! Watch where you're going," she called as she turned a bit to see who had practically run over her. There was a woman hurrying away, hastily turning from her. Kristine thought she may have looked nervous, maybe distracted. She also knew if she didn't get out of the street she'd be fair game for traffic when the light changed. New York was always in a hurry. The people walked with a purpose - like they always had someplace to be and were hell-bent on getting there. Kristine could relate to that.

Once across the street, she looked down at her white, spaghetti strap top. There were no signs of coffee stains, and it was still neatly tucked into her navy and white pinstriped skirt. It was too hot for her suit jacket, which was draped over her bag.

"You're here early today," Ed the security guard said as she walked past his desk. Ed was probably 80 years old and resembled Yoda more than the Terminator. Ed wasn't going to stop anyone who wanted to come into the building. He had a nightstick, a walkie talkie and a case of bursitis.

"Good morning, Ed. You know you say that to me every day," Kristine called back as she walked into a waiting elevator. She pushed her sunglasses back on top of her head. She punched the button for the 17th floor, sipped her coffee and wondered why anyone bothered to remove the 13 from the buttons. If 13 was truly a bad number, did it matter there was no button? The poor fools on the 14th floor were still on the 13th floor no mater what you called it. She sighed, took another drink of her coffee and thought how silly the superstitious could be.

The elevator car dinged, and the doors opened. The lights on the floor were on. They were always on. No one ever bothered to turn them off when they left. Of course, she thought, the evening shift, which was mostly copy editors, left only hours before the reporters showed up in the morning. She walked down the hall past the desks piled high with old newspapers, files, books and other materials that would make that person seem busy. The thing about being a reporter is you could take off during the day chasing a "lead" and actually be in the park playing Frisbee - well, unless you had an assignment and a deadline. Kristine was sure there were people who did this, but she wasn't one of them. If she didn't have an assignment, she would listen to police scanners waiting for something interesting or start going over public records looking for something - anything - that would make a good story.

She rounded the corner and headed for her desk. This was the best time of the day - when Burt Newman wasn't in the office. Burt was a slob. He was the stereotypical news guy from the movies times 10. He always had coffee dribbled down his shirt and white stuff collecting in the corner of his mouth. She took a second to consider what that white stuff was…never mind, she thought. She didn't want to know. Burt's belly lapped over the top of his pants, and his shirt gapped between the buttons over his midsection. His ties were always too short and didn't match the rest of his attire, which usually consisted of a cream colored, short sleeve shirt, which in the past decade had most likely been white. Yellow arm pit stains accessorized the shirt. She considered the stains proof Burt rarely, if ever, bothered with antiperspirant. He must have either had a closet full of brown, polyester pants with a thick waistband absent of belt loops, or he wore the same pair over and over. She shuddered at the thought.

It gets worse. Burt was crowned with gray, greasy hairs. Well, maybe there was just one long hair he wrapped around his head over and over again. His black, thick-framed glasses had a coating of gunk on the lenses that probably impaired his vision. These were the trademark fashions of Burt Newman. If that wasn't bad enough, his personality wasn't exactly congenial either.

If there was a group of people about whom Burt could be intolerant, he was. He said America was being taken over by foreigners. No amount of arguing about how anyone who wasn't Native American was a foreigner, or how one of the strengths of the USA was the fact it was built on the blending of so many different cultures could convince him otherwise. The only thing Kristine had in common with Burt was a stubborn streak and a dislike of each other.

Perhaps even more annoying than his lack of hygiene and perverse attitude about people was the way he pounded on a keyboard as if the added pressure on the keys would give his words more emphasis. He mumbled to himself as he beat up the alphabet. Kristine couldn't hear herself think when Burt's words flowed. She was convinced people went on the record with Burt simply to get rid of him. If she was correct, that would be the only plus side to being that repulsive. For all the turmoil Burt brought to her life, his stories usually ended up buried deep inside the paper or held over for a slow news day.

She put her bag and coffee on her desk and noticed a bulge in the front pocket of the bag. Reaching in, she pulled out a disc. There was nothing written on it, which meant it wasn't hers. She always labeled her discs. She took out the laptop and clicked it into the docking station. She leaned back in her chair and waited for the computer screen to go through the flashing it took to get to her main screen.

Suddenly she noticed a pungent smell. She felt her face crinkle as she sat upright and looked around.

"What the hell is that smell?" she said out loud to no one. She looked across her neat, clean desk over to the piles of chaos. It had to be Newman. No one irritated her quite like he did. She stood and walked around to his desk. She took a pencil from one of the stacks and used it to move some of the debris. There it was - a half eaten tuna salad sandwich. The only thing that smelled worse than fresh tuna was tuna salad that had been sitting out for God knows how long. She didn't know what shocked her more; that Burt had left half a sandwich uneaten or that he was just that much of a slob. She put the eraser of the pencil on the paper holding the sandwich and dragged it to the edge of the desk where she had Burt's garbage can ready to catch it as it fell. She dropped the pencil in with it and took the garbage can down the hall to the Sports Department. Most of those guys traveled, and the rest wouldn't be in until later in the day. Plus, they may not even notice it, she thought. She stopped by the ladies' room to wash her hands just in case she caught any Burt cooties.

When she got back to her desk, she pulled out the can of disinfectant she kept in her top drawer and sprayed Burt's desk and chair and then her own. She shook her head and considered what it would be like to sit across from someone who didn't require you to decontaminate your work area on a daily basis. She put the can back into the desk drawer and closed it. She sat back down, picked up the disc and looked at it. Could someone have mistaken their bag for hers last night?

She thought back to the previous evening. She had been finishing a story about city workers drinking on the job and the dangers to the public and then filed it from home. The disc wasn't in her bag last night when she arrived at her apartment, because she remembered removing a business card she had received earlier in the day. She had to have gotten this disc somewhere between her apartment and the office this morning. Maybe someone in the coffee shop gave it to her, but she was still too tired to remember sliding it into the pocket. Then she remembered the lady in the crosswalk. She closed her eyes to remember what she looked like. She looked like she was in a hurry, which didn't set her apart from any other New Yorker. "Think," she muttered to herself. "You get paid to notice details." She shook her head. The only other things she remembered were the woman had brown hair, wore sunglasses and seemed anxious. Again - not unlike most of the population of the city. Her cell phone rang. She looked at the number and recognized it as Derrick. He was her closest friend.

"Hey, what's up?" she asked.

"Girl, I just got off the late shift. Meet me for breakfast and a facial - my skin looks like hell with these bags under my eyes." Derrick was a nurse and usually worked the emergency room. Kristine had met him while working stories - waiting for patient updates and trying to talk to family members of victims. Derrick was gorgeous and gay.

"Can't. Sorry. Gotta work," she said staring at her screen. "Meet for dinner?"

"Can't. Gotta date."

"Who?"

"Dr. Feelgood," he said triumphantly. Kristine smiled and sat up in her chair.

"No you don't."

"Oh yes I do."

"I thought he told you he was straight."

"Turns out he couldn't resist this."

"Well, congratulations! You have to tell me all about it. Where's he taking you?"

"Don't know. Don't care. I'm outta here. I'm giving

myself the spa treatment today. I may even get a bikini wax," he said.

"Don't let them wax your eyebrows again. Remember the last time? You looked like an idiot."

"Impossible," he said laughing. "See you later, my dear!"

"Have fun and call me later," she said disconnecting and putting her phone on her desk.

She put the disc into the computer and clicked open the drive. There was a document at the top that read, "1 Read me first" along with several other files all numbered. Kristine double clicked on the first document.

> Ms. Larkin,
>
> I took your name from the newspaper stories you've written. I don't know if I can trust you, but I know I can't trust anyone else. That's why I can't tell you who I am. I also need to protect my son and his family.
>
> This disc has information you can use to start an investigation. I can tell you're ambitious, so I know you are the right person to do this. This information may get both of us killed, so you need to be very careful.
>
> I hope to live long enough to see the story in print.

The note wasn't signed. Kristine read it three times. Her heart was beating fast and her mouth was dry. Without taking her eyes off the screen, she reached for her now cold coffee. As she put the cup back on her desk, she started clicking on the documents and read them in order. She wasn't sure what she was hoping to find, but she knew what she had didn't make sense to her. Some documents had what looked like code names and numbers next to them, some looked like shipping orders and some were memos that were obviously in some sort of code. She had something that looked like bank records and a couple of seemingly unrelated headlines that most likely came from news stories. The stories weren't anything she had written. She scribbled a few notes in her notepad. She looked around the newsroom. A few more reporters had arrived. She ripped out the page of her notebook, crumbled it and threw it in her garbage can. Should she even leave it there? She reached in and pulled it out.

"This is ridiculous," she mumbled to herself. For all she knew this was a practical joke played on her by coworkers who wanted her to chase a bogus lead. Still, there was a line from the letter about protecting family that tore at her. She closed the disc so no one could see it on her screen. She slowly walked to the paper shredder and fed the notepaper through the little slit. By the time she got back to her desk, Burt had waddled in and plopped into his chair. Her mind was so preoccupied with the disc she forgot to be upset at his presence.

"What's wrong with you, Little Girl," Burt asked. Kristine had complained to Human Resources about the names, but Burt was definitely an old dog and he wouldn't learn the trick of civility. Kristine couldn't manage to put the effort into being flirty with him - there was nothing in it for her.

"It seems as though most of my problems involve sitting across from you, Newman," she said in retort. She had to admit, she almost enjoyed their verbal sparing from time to time. It kept her on her toes, and she was often pleased when she came up with something so witty it shut up Burt.

"Did the princess start the day on the wrong side of the bed? Maybe if you were prettier you would have someone in it to stop you from rolling that far," Burt said with a snort of pride at his retort.

"Write anything that actually made it into the paper lately?" she said in a superior tone as she picked up her cell phone and pretended to call someone. She had been called many things, but ugly wasn't one. She dialed her home number and started talking before the machine kicked on to play her recorded message. She thought she heard Burt mumble the word "bitch" as he looked for his pencil.

After her five minute, one-way conversation with the answering machine, she closed the phone and put it on her desk. She was desperate to open the disc again, but she didn't want to do it now. Not with prying eyes. The newspaper business is very competitive. She removed the disc from the computer and slid it into an envelope. She carried the envelope with her to the Editor-in-Chief's office.

William Montgomery was a southern gentleman who earned the title of editor-in-chief by working his way up the corporate ladder from being a clerk. His family's money and influence could have gotten him there much faster. He was the type of man who believed in hard work, and no one could ever accuse him of taking any favors.

Will was the person who had the final decision whether Kristine was hired. She had interviewed with other editors on the newspaper, but she felt quite sure Will had requested an interview with her. She knew she caught his eye as she toured the newsroom, just as he had caught hers. He was tall - maybe 6'4, handsome and dressed in designer clothes. His dark blond hair showed signs of graying. He had the slender body of a distance runner, and his dimples were enough to make any woman melt. He gave the impression that every line on his face was hard earned. He was the anti-Burt. Will spoke with a slight hint of a southern drawl and an intelligence that made Kristine envious. Kristine was young, impetuous and always focused on the end result. Will saw the big picture. Will was more deliberate and thoughtful in his actions. She recognized he had a maturity that she hoped she would gain with age and experience. She sometimes even caught herself trying to think like Will in situations. That's what she needed now that she had this disc.

Will's secretary sat outside his office like a lioness protecting her young complete with long red nails that looked like they were painted with the blood of the last person who tried to get in to see him without an appointment. Joyce didn't like Kristine - that was obvious from day one. Joyce had a Lurch-from-the-Addams-Family quality to her. There wasn't a feminine feature in her pale, sunken face. "Hey, Joyce," Kristine said whimsically as she walked into the office. Kristine stood about 5'10 with her 2 ½" heels, but Joyce still had a couple of inches on her and probably about 70 pounds.

"He's busy," Joyce said only briefly looking away from her computer screen to see Kristine. She made a disapproving sound with her mouth. Kristine glanced down at her attire and wondered what caused the reproachful noise this time. The skirt? No. It hit her at the knee, and Joyce couldn't see that anyway. Was it the spaghetti strap shirt? Hm…maybe. It showed her shoulders and scooped lower than what Joyce would probably deem acceptable. Kristine instinctively pushed out her modest chest to add to Joyce's annoyance.

"Can you at least let him know I'm here to see him?" Kristine asked calmly. "It's important." She was more focused on the disc than verbally sparing with Joyce.

"Isn't it always, dear?" Joyce replied in a scolding tone. That was pretty much it for Kristine.

"Yes, Joyce. I try to keep our social visits to a minimum, so if I'm here, it's important," Kristine grew agitated about Joyce's dismissal of her. In Kristine's mind, Joyce didn't believe she had anything important to say. Joyce picked up the phone and buzzed Will.

"I'm sorry to bother you. Kristine Larkin is here to see you. I told her you were..." Joyce looked at Kristine with a disappointed expression. "Yes Sir." She put down the phone. "You can go in," she said in defeat and returned to her computer screen.

Kristine walked into Will's office. He was behind his desk reading this morning's edition. He raised his eyes and looked over his glasses at her.

"Your pit bull needs to be put on a leash," Kristine said as she swung the door closed behind her.

"Good morning to you, too," Will said as he removed the glasses and put them on his desk. "Nice job on the bank robbery story. What can I do for you?" Kristine had already sat down in the chair across from him. She was looking at the envelope she was holding in her pin-stripped lap and wishing she had thought more about what she would say once she was in this chair.

"I think I'd like some time to do some investigating on a lead I got this morning," she said. "It may take some time to flesh out the story, and I'd like to be 100% dedicated to it."

"What lead?"

"Uh, it's this disc someone gave me. Not much to go on yet, but I'd like to look into it."

"A disc? Who gave it to you?"

"I, uh, I'm not sure."

Will leaned back in his chair, rested his elbows on the chair arms and put the tips of his fingers together. She felt like she needed to say something else. She searched her mind for words. She hated when he did this - she wanted to know what he was thinking.

"So, I have some information that I just want to look into.

It's not a big deal. Or, well, it could be a big deal depending on what I find. Will you say something now? I hate awkward silence."

Her mind flashed back to her interview with Will. He sat there silently watching her answer questions. He didn't take notes - just sat there with his finger tips touching. She hid her nervousness so well she thought she might have even amused him. She wore a black suit that looked like it had been tailored for her. The skirt ended just above the knee and the white blouse under the jacket was opened just far enough to be professional but still draw some attention. She may have accidentally let her skirt ride up her leg a little farther when she sat down and crossed her legs. She may have leaned over a little more than necessary when she reached for her clippings in her bag. She may have even twirled a wisp of hair that had fallen from the clip in a slightly flirtatious way - subtle yet detectable. She was so attracted to him she almost lost sight of the reason she was sitting in front of him. He stared at her while she spoke. He seemed relaxed and confident. If he had picked up on any of her flirtations, he didn't say anything or make any kind of knowing gesture. Unlike the young men at college, he was mature and a gentleman. She wasn't sure she knew what to say to him or how to say it. He threw her off balance, and she wasn't used to that.

She honestly thought she had gotten the interview by mistake. She went to a school at a small college in the Mid-West and had no experience other than working for school newspapers. Still, she knew she had talent and sent her clips and resume to the Chronicle along with most other newspapers in the country. She certainly never expected to get the most sought after job in journalism, but here she was sitting in front of Will this time as his employee.

"Ah, Krissy," he said in a thoughtful tone. Family

members were the only other people she allowed to call her Krissy. "If most anyone else would have walked through that door asking for cart blanche, I would have asked that person to shut the door on the way out," he sighed. "But you have an amazing instinct for recognizing a story and an angle."

"Is that a yes?" she asked eagerly. Will had come to trust her instincts and writing but told her in a recent review of her work that she was still learning to be a great investigator. There was a pause as they looked at each other. He's married and the father of twin girls, she reminded herself. She caught herself biting her bottom lip as she studied him and blinked her eyes hard to clear the unprofessional thoughts.

"You're asking me to tell the rest of our staff, editors and the publisher of the paper that our rising star is off doing God-knows-what for God-knows-how-long. I need more to tell them."

"You can't!" She moved forward in her seat. "Will, you can't tell anyone what I'm doing. Just tell them I have a big lead."

"Kris, this is a business. Things don't exactly operate like that."

"I know, and honestly, this may pan out to be nothing. I just have a feeling this is going to go somewhere huge," she could feel her eyes grow bigger in a begging expression.

"I'll have to tell them something. I'll handle it, but this had better be good," he said leaning forward to put his elbows on his desk.

"So, this means I'm good to go?" she replied eagerly.

"It means I'll give you some time." Her excitement grew, but she didn't know exactly why. She didn't know what was going to happen next, and all she had to go on was a disc that didn't make any sense. "On some conditions," he said with authority. He stood, walked around the desk and leaned up

13

against it so he was standing over her. She looked up at him and waited to hear what he had to say. "One is you will come to me for help if you need it." She nodded. "Two - you will give me regular updates on your progress or lack thereof. You may not want me to report to the chain of command, but I want to know everything." She nodded again, but she wasn't sure she meant this one. "One more, I'll give you two months. If at the end of two months you still don't have anything solid, you'll give up this lead." She nodded again.

"You won't regret this, Will," she said standing and touching his arm without thinking about it first. She pulled her hand away quickly and made her way to the door fighting the urge to run out of the office. His eyes followed her - she could feel them.

"I sure hope not," he said returning to his seat and picking up his reading glasses. She blew Joyce a kiss as she breezed past and rushed to her desk. She packed her laptop and put the disc securely in the bag.

"Where's the fire, Little Girl?" Burt asked, watching her from behind the junk yard he called his desk.

"Some of us actually work around here," she said looking around to make sure she wasn't forgetting anything. Afraid of what Burt might have done to her coffee while unattended, she tossed the remaining few drinks in the garbage.

"Some of us actually earned the right to work here," he said snorting again.

"Yes. Some of us have. You, I'm sure, were hired and retained out of pity," she grabbed her suit jacket off the back of her chair and headed for the door. She tried not to point at Burt and yell, "In your face, loser!"

As she walked to the elevator, she thought about how competitive she was. She always had to win. She even cheated at Candyland when she was a kid. Sometimes it served her well - like her drive to accomplish great things in her career, but it didn't server her so well in her personal life. Who cares, she thought. She hoped her winning spirit wouldn't let her down now. This story could be her Pulitzer. It could be her book deal, her opportunity to be on talk shows and her opportunity to "in your face" all the people she didn't like in high school and college, especially the person she saw as her biggest competition - Tara Tierra.

That wasn't even her real name. Her real name was Tara Butmacher. No one blamed her for changing it as soon as she turned 18 years old. Tierra actually suited Tara physically. She was perfect. Perfect skin and her hair never moved. Tara grew up across town from Kristine. Her dad had money - a lot of it. Tara and Kristine competed against each other in tennis matches from the time they were seven or eight years old through high school. Then, while in high school, they competed against each other in journalism. Tara always beat Kristine in tennis, but Kristine always beat Tara at journalism. Kristine won some recognition for her work in college, but she was always in a different division because of her smaller, less prestigious school. Tara went to a very old, highly respected and expensive college (thanks to Mr. Butmacher's fortune) and landed a very good job being a weekend anchor, or news reader as Kristine liked to call her, at one of New York's lower rated stations. Tara would do an occasional feature on the evening news, but she didn't get the hard news stories.

While Kristine considered Tara a pain in her butt from day one, she wondered if she ever even registered a blip on Tara's radar. Of course, Kristine couldn't completely blame herself for disliking Tara. Females, even Tara's friends, typically disliked Tara.

Tara was untouchable. She had shiny blonde hair, big blue eyes and skin like a porcelain doll. She was one of those people who didn't seem to sweat. At the end of a grueling three set tennis match Kristine would be drenched with perspiration, ponytail soaked with no makeup left. Tara still looked like she had just walked onto the court. Now that they were both in New York, Kristine had the more prestigious job, but Tara was the one people recognized when they saw her walking down the street.

Someday Tara may have to report on what a huge success Kristine had made of herself, she thought. Tara would ask what it was like to be recognized as one of the best journalist in the world, and Kristine would blush bashfully and answer with the perfect humble response, "I'm just trying to make the world a better place for our children." Kristine smiled to herself as the elevator doors opened to the lobby. It was a good daydream that she would make come true someday. But first, she had to get this story. She burst through the doors of the building determined to do just that.

Chapter Two

The next two months were filled with excitement - sometimes good, sometimes scary. The good excitement brought leads as she closed in on more and more facts about the story she chased. The scary brought calls to her apartment late at night, a broken lock on her desk drawer in the newsroom, a near miss with a car in a cross-walk, and she was pretty sure someone had broken into her apartment. She had arrived home one night and things were just not right - nothing obvious but an item here or there had been moved. At first she chalked these events up to paranoia, but eventually she conceded these weren't just coincidence.

On the morning of the two month deadline given by Will, Kristine left her second floor apartment and stood a match up against the corner of the door. It was a little trick she had learned from a TV show, but it let her know if anyone entered her apartment. She began the ritual after the potential break-in.

It was a gloomy, crisp fall morning - the kind of morning when the dampness from the last night's rain made the air feel colder than it was. She left her building and walked the six blocks to work. She considered the 12 blocks to and from work (and any other walking she did to tail a lead) her exercise for the day. She didn't like to sweat - not even when she was playing tennis trying to get scholarship money, and she certainly didn't see the benefit of the phrase, "No pain, no gain." The only thing she liked less than sweating was pain. She would see people jogging on the streets, and they never looked like they were enjoying themselves.

Feeling threatened made avoiding pain an even more important part of Kristine's life. She changed her schedule often so she had no routine. She went to work during the busiest time of the morning now. Instead of comments about being early, Ed the security guard made comments about her sleeping late or keeping banker's hours. Burt Newman was beating her into the office on some mornings - a first since she began at the paper three years ago.

She also felt the need to perform security checks when she got to her desk. She knew better than to keep anything important in her desk or at her apartment so whoever broke into them wouldn't find any of her work. She checked the drawers of her desk and around the lock for scratches. She put a piece of clear tape along the side of her drawers so she could tell if they had been opened. Everything seemed okay.

"Don't worry, Little Girl. No one cares what you have in your desk," Burt Newman snarled from across his desk.

"Mind your own business, Burt," she said as she docked her computer.

"The princess is paranoid," said Burt amused.

"You know, if you spent half as much time on your personal hygiene as you do trying to piss me off, you wouldn't be so repulsive to look at and smell. You must have to hold your wife captive so she can't escape or is she a pathetic mess like you are," she snapped. As the words came out of her mouth, she was sorry. Her sparring had never gotten so personal or so mean. She saw from the look on his face she had hurt him. "I'm sorry, Burt."

"I expect as much from you," he said and walked away from his desk. She buried her face in her hands and rubbed her temples. Her phone rang. She saw from the extension it was Joyce.

"Hello?"

"Mr. Montgomery would like to see you."

"I'll be right there." Her hand shook a little as she put down the phone. She stood up and picked up her bag, a note pad and a pen. She tried to think of something nice to say to Joyce. It also dawned on her how many people disliked her in that office. The men in the Sports Department liked her, she consoled herself. She sighed - that's because she flirted with them. They weren't competition for her. At the office holiday party (you aren't allowed to call them Christmas parties anymore) last year, she spent the night hanging out with them - probably because no one else wanted to talk to her. Well, except Will. Most of the men who worked at the paper were married. Most of the men who worked in the Sports Department were divorced. Following a baseball team all season could take its toll on a marriage. She was a competition and focal point for male bonding for the men in Sports. They could say and do all the typical guys-tripped-out-on-testosterone things guys like to do when they're together without her protesting, and she enjoyed the playful flirting. Her run-ins with the guys in Sports were rare because of their schedules, but they did a lot to boost her ego.

To everyone else at the paper, she was a pain in the ass. She always blamed them, though. After her exchange with Burt Newman this morning, maybe she was more of the problem than she cared to admit, she thought. Will was in Joyce's work area when Kristine arrived, which prevented any of the niceties she hadn't had time to plan.

"Kris, come on in," Will said. Kristine just waved at Joyce, a gesture Joyce probably mistook for sarcasm. Will closed the door behind Kristine. She plopped down in one of the chairs across from him. Will's office was almost the size of her apartment. He had a sitting area, 47 inch TV, his own restroom, a little stainless steel refrigerator and a huge, decorative cherry wood desk. He sat in his black leather chair. It was the kind of chair that would have made anyone else look small. "What's wrong?"

"Nothing, why?" she asked.

"You've been in my office for 30 seconds and haven't said a word," he said sitting back.

"I'd like to move my desk away from Burt's," she replied quietly.

"You've asked me to do this three or four times now and the answer is always no," he said.

"Today's different," she said. "I was really mean to him."

"You're always really mean to him. You're mean to everyone except me and the guys in Sports. That's why no one wants to sit near you," he said amused. She cringed at his words. She thought for a minute and realized she should probably tell him what had happened before anyone else did.

"I kind of went over the line this time, Will. I kind of attacked him and his wife," she said. Will closed his eyes for a moment before opening them again.

"What did you say?"

"I said he was repulsive and he probably had to hold his wife captive so she wouldn't escape from him unless she was just as bad as he is," she said and sighed. Instinctively, she felt the need to defend herself. "But he is repulsive. You'd have to admit that. And he's always picking on me, calling me 'little girl' and you know how much I hate that!"

"Let me tell you something, but I'd like for you not to repeat it," Will said leaning forward in his chair his voice deep as usual but with an almost scolding tone she hadn't heard in the past. "Burt's wife lost both of her legs and her eyesight as a complication of diabetes. Burt spends all of his money and energy taking care of her. During the day, he pays for a nurse to come in and help her. The medical expenses, the nurse and taking care of her are taking their toll on him. I think he likes you, because you don't treat him like you feel sorry for him." Tears welled up in her eyes.

"Crap," she whispered.

"Now, let's forget we had that conversation. I want to know what's going on with the story," he said leaning back in the chair again. "We haven't talked in a week." She cleared her throat and tried to erase what she had just heard from her mind.

"Do you have a radio in here?" she asked looking around and feeling two inches tall. She walked over to the TV and picked up the remote. She stepped back, pointed it at the TV and clicked the power button. The television was set to a 24 hour news channel, which she didn't take the time to identify. She pushed the volume button to create background noise. She motioned for Will to come around his desk and join her on the sofa closer to the TV. He did, and they sat facing each other.

"I have a strong story," she said. "But it's not great, yet. I'm sure there's more out there. I brought you this," she stood up and turned away from him. She untucked her shirt and reached under her blouse to retrieve a disc. She put the disc in her mouth and tucked her white button-down shirt into the black dress pants. She didn't consider herself a fashionista, but she knew what looked good and stylish on her. She took the disc from her mouth and turned around to see a highly amused, yet very concerned look on Will's face. She sat down and put the disc on her leg. "I need you to keep this somewhere really safe and do *not* tell *anyone* you have it." He was looking at the disc.

"You're off the story," he said quietly looking up at her. This brought the life back into her.

"What?!" she said practically jumping off the couch and the disc fell onto the floor. She picked up the shiny circle and held her work between her thumb and index finger.

"If you're walking around with your story stuffed under your clothes and turning on background noise, you obviously think there's some sort of danger," he said taking her arm and pulling her back down on the sofa. "Why?" She searched her mind for something to say. "Tell me why or I'm completely killing the story," he said.

"Okay, just don't kill the story," she said unconsciously putting her hand on his leg. She realized where her hand was and drew it away quickly. "Sorry," she said as she felt her face grow warm. "I noticed the lock on my desk broken one morning when I came into the office."

"And?" he replied. Kristine wondered if he had some sort of magic powers that let him read her mind - like a Jedi or something.

"And someone *may* have broken into my apartment."

"And?"

"And someone *may* have tried to run me down in a crosswalk," she said putting extra emphasis on the word "may."

"Run you down?" he asked shocked and panicked. "Why is this the first time I'm hearing about it?"

"Hey, this is New York. People get nearly run over in crosswalks every day," she said somewhat surprised at his reaction.

"This isn't a joke, Krissy. No story is worth losing your life."

"What life," she said sarcastically. "Will, in case you haven't noticed, this job is my life." They stared at each other for a moment.

"You're driven," he said comfortingly. "This is my fault. A lot of pressure came with the job offer, but you've surpassed even my expectations as a reporter. You're young. You have a lot of life left to live." He didn't sound like an editor. He sounded like a friend. She didn't know what to say to this.

"I really want this story, Will."

"I know you do. But you don't want it for the right reasons. You don't want to uncover some truth to right a wrong. You want to win. You want to be first," he said now sounding more like a father - or worse…a psychiatrist. Still, there was truth in his words. "Let me give the story to someone else."

"No, you can't do that to me," she nearly shouted gripping the disc tighter. "I don't want you to understand my motives. I've done a hell of a lot of work on this, and it's mine. Giving it to someone else will only take the focus off of me and put it on someone else. Do you want that?" She knew she had a point, but now she was afraid he'd totally kill the story. "Will, if you take away my story, I'll quit and sell it to someone else," she said without thinking. She couldn't tell if he was impressed, hurt or disappointed by that threat.

"You're not leaving me much choice here," he said. They sat in silence, the only noise coming from an update of the stock market on the news, for what seemed like a few minutes. "How close are you to getting what you need?"

"Close," she said. She didn't know this for sure, but it was a gut feeling she had had for a few days.

"Here's what we're going to do," he said standing. He paced for a few seconds (he did this when he was deep in thought) before he sat down again. "Okay. We're going to put you into a higher security apartment. You're to do as much as you can via email and phone calls. I don't want you to leave the building unless it's absolutely necessary, and you will not leave alone. I'll hire around the clock security."

"Will, don't you think that's overkill? I don't need a bodyguard," she said uncomfortable at the thought someone would be babysitting her but curiously finding it intriguing that he wanted to take care of her.

"No. I don't," he said. She knew she wouldn't win an

argument with him. Her mind raced as she feigned listening to him as he continued to give her instructions about how to live her life. She spent most of the day in his office going over story details with him, and he received a delivery of a large sum of cash. He gave it to her so she wouldn't have to use credit cards should the need arise for her to leave town. He also received a delivery of a new cell phone which he gave to her. By the time 6:00 arrived, she didn't know if she felt safer or more panicked with him helping her. The only thing left for her to do was get some of her stuff out of her apartment, but Will told her he had someone run out to buy her what she needed, and everything would be waiting for her.

Will led her from his office, and she nearly had to run to keep pace with him. He led her to a set of elevators she had never ridden before today. After a walk down a strange hallway and another elevator ride, she was in a parking garage. It was dark - probably underground, she thought. Will was quiet as he concentrated and looked nervously around the garage.

"Remind me to get someone to take care of the security footage," he said without looking at her.

"Right," she replied and rolled her eyes. Total overkill, she thought.

Will pushed a button on his keychain and the hazard lights on a black Lexus LS sedan flashed. He walked to the passenger side. She followed, but he opened the back door.

"Get in," he ordered, and she realized she was waiting for him to open the front door. She opened her mouth to say something, and he added, "Please." She got into the backseat of the car. He closed the door and walked around to the driver's side of the car. She looked around. The car was spotless inside and out. The leather was cool, even through her clothing. He turned the key in the ignition, and the car was so quiet she wasn't even sure it started until he pulled out of the parking space.

"Stay down," he ordered again.

"Will, the windows are tinted," she said in a deadpan tone.

"Humor me," he urged. She curled up on the backseat. Traffic in the city was bumper to bumper. Will nervously watched the rearview mirror. After a half hour of being curled up, she started to feel achy. She sat up slightly.

"Look, this is crazy," she said. He didn't respond. "Are you ignoring me?"

"I don't want it to look like I'm talking to anyone," he said. She thought he was kind of silly playing this cloak and dagger spy game. She humored him and put her head down on the seat. She closed her eyes and imagined how this was probably the most excitement he had seen in years.

Kristine met his wife Emily Wentworth-Montgomery once when she brought the twin girls in for Will's 25th anniversary working at the paper. She seemed as uptight as her name. She had blonde hair cut into a shoulder length bob with a headband holding her hair away from her face. Not one hair was out of place. Not even a fly-away. "How do you control fly-aways?" she thought. Never mind. Emily smiled at all the right times and intensely monitored the kids as they ate their cake. Heaven forbid they get blue icing on their white, wrinkle-free dresses.

The girls looked like dolls. They barely spoke a word and smiled at the right times, too. When they posed for a family photo, it looked like something you'd get when you bought the frame. Picture perfect - too perfect. Kristine wondered if Emily Wentworth-Montgomery ever passed gas. The thought made her giggle out loud.

"What's so funny back there," Will asked. Kristine hadn't noticed, but the car was moving quickly.

"Oh nothing," she said and wondered how long she had been lost in thought. The car pulled into a parking lot, or at least that is what it felt like as the motion sent her rocking back and forth on the seat.

"Can I get up now?" she asked.

"Wait until I get into the garage," he said concentrating. She waited until the car pulled into a spot and came to a stop. Will released the latch on the trunk from the inside and got out. She sat up and rolled her stiff neck. Will opened the door and held his hand out to her. She took it and got out of the car with her purse and laptop bag. She looked down at his hand in hers. She wasn't sure they had purposely touched since the first day of work when he welcomed her to the office. He let go of her hand and moved to the trunk. He removed some bags. They seemed to be new, black luggage - must be her store-bought items. There were too many for him to carry on his own, so she took some from him. They walked to a door, and Will flashed a badge in front of a reader. "This is a high security building," he said and opened the door for her.

"Yeah. Thanks," she said as she moved through the door. There was a bank of mirrored elevators in the hall. He pushed the up arrow. She deduced there must be more levels of garage below them. They stepped into the elevators when the doors opened and turned around to face them again. Will slid a key into the opening next to the highest floor. "Wow. Penthouse? Nice." Will didn't say anything. They rode the elevator to the top floor and stepped off into a very nice apartment or maybe it was a condo. Either way, it was beautiful. "You know, this place is going to make it difficult to go back to the closet I call an apartment. Whose place is this?"

"Mine," Will said as he carried bags around a corner. She crinkled her eyebrows and repeated what he said. She hadn't realized how hungry she was until she saw the kitchen. She tried to remember if she had eaten anything, but the day seemed like it had been a week long. She put the bags she was carrying on a huge white, overstuffed chair. Everything seemed to be white, black or red - very masculine. Will came back around the corner. "I put your bags in the spare room," he said and walked to the kitchen. "Hungry?" She was confused.

"Um, yeah," she said and followed him into the kitchen. "Will? Won't your wife be upset I'm here?" She didn't know where Will and his family lived and hadn't really considered a place like this.

"Emily and I are no longer together," he said while opening the refrigerator. "How about Italian?"

"How about Italian? You just tell me you and your wife are separated and then go into the dinner question like it's nothing," she said as she closed the refrigerator and stood face to face with him. He was tall...maybe even taller than she thought. "I'm really sorry, Will."

"It's okay. It's for the best," he said looking down at her. "Now, do you like Italian? If you're not hungry, I am." To Kristine, Italian meant ravioli from a can or pizza take out.

"Italian is fine with me. What can I do to help?" she asked watching him pull out a pot and put it under the sink. She wanted more information on the separation. She tried to ignore the reporter questions spinning like a huge, mid-western tornado through her already over-burdened mind.

He was her boss. Their relationship was strictly professional, and she should keep it that way, right? What if he poured his heart out to her and starting crying about how much he missed his wife and kids? Would she be able to look at him the same way in the newsroom? The answer was no. She didn't want to break her image of him. That made it easier to let the twister of questions rise back into the clouds.

"Just make yourself at home," he said. She turned and walked around the counter to the other side of the wall and sat on a bar stool to watch him. The kitchen cabinets were white, the granite countertops were black and the walls were painted a deep red. He took a bottle of wine from a wine rack on top of the refrigerator and put it on the counter. He slid two wine glasses off the rack hanging from under one of the cabinets. He put them on the counter next to the wine and then opened the bottle with ease. When Kristine opened a bottle of wine, it looked more like a wrestling match. The bottles she opened had bits of cork floating in them by the time she was finished.

He poured the wine, twirled it so it could coat the glass and then smelled it. She was mesmerized by him. He was the most sophisticated man she had ever known. He took a sip, put the glass down and then poured one for her. She took a drink, and he smiled as he watched her.

"What," she asked smiling back. She went to take another drink.

"That's what I love about you," he said, and she choked on her wine. She coughed several times and couldn't tell if her face was red from coughing or what he had said. "You're not pretentious. Are you okay?"

"Yeah," she said as she took the napkin he handed to her. She dabbed at the tears in the corner of her eyes. "Just went down the wrong pipe," she added. He smiled at her again and went back to making dinner. She ran through the remark again and again. Harmless - she decided. He said "that's what I love about you" just like people say, "I'm going to kill you" or "I could just die." Yep. That was it, she thought a little disappointed and a little relieved. She took another drink of wine - a bigger one. She started some small talk about where he learned to cook - he was making spaghetti sauce using tomatoes and fresh herbs and things she didn't even recognize.

He put a couple of black plates, knives, forks, spoons and red cloth napkins on the counter.

"Want to set the table for me?" he asked.

"Sure," she said and stood. She started setting the glass table, and he refilled her wine glass.

"Hey, don't forget these," he said and put a plate of Italian bread, a small dish with olive oil in it and matches on the counter. She thought a moment about why they needed matches. She turned around and saw candles on the table. No big deal. So he likes candles burning while he eats. Only the wicks were still white all the way to the tip. He picked up the matches and came out of the kitchen. "I'll get these," he said. He walked past her to the table and lit each candle. His aftershave hung in the air as he went past. Nice.

She tried not to look confused and picked up the remaining items on the counter. "It will be ready in a minute," he said and went back to the kitchen.

The sleeves of Will's white dress shirt were rolled up to the elbow. She'd never realized he only wore white dress shirts until now. Despite the dicing of tomatoes, herbs and all of the other ingredients she didn't recognize, he didn't have a drop of anything on this clothing. This is how Tara Butmacher would look if she was cooking, Kristine decided with a sly smile. The smile died when she realized what she looked like on the rare occasion she had tried to cook. She'd once had to wash her hair twice to get everything out of it. She was never going to be like Tara, Emily Wentworth-Montgomery or Will. She crossed her arms in front of her as she felt an inferiority complex trying to emerge.

"Shake it off," she told herself. "You'll be here for what? A couple of days tops. Then you can go back to your normal life. The story will run, everyone will admire and adore you and the fact you get messy when you cook - or even the fact you can't cook - will seem charming." She felt better already and unfolded her arms. She even smiled with a feeling of self-satisfaction.

Dinner was fabulous - better than anything Kristine had ever had in a restaurant. Of course, after paying her outrageous rent for the extremely modest apartment, there wasn't much left of her paycheck for fancy dining - at least not the kind of restaurants Will was probably used to patronizing.

Half way through dinner, Will opened another bottle of wine. The wine relaxed her, and they talked like two old friends about current events, world affairs and the city in which they worked. Neither of them brought up anything too personal.

After dinner, they cleared the dishes and went to the living room with their glasses and the bottle of wine. Will sat on the big white sofa and Kristine sat on the ground next to him.

"What are you doing down there?" he asked.

"The wine. I want to be closer to the floor if I fall down," she said, and they both laughed out loud.

"Good idea," he said and shifted from the sofa to the floor. She was feeling tipsy and brave.

"You know, I never thought I'd get a job at your paper," she said and took another sip.

"I knew you'd get a job at my paper as soon as I saw you touring the newsroom," he said and looked down at his wine glass. "You're a beautiful addition to any room." Luckily, she wasn't drinking when he said that or wine would have shot across the room. Alarms sounded in her mind.

"The only reason I got the job is because you liked the way I looked?" She felt her temper begin to scorch her face.

"Oh no," he looked down in embarrassment. "I wouldn't have offered the interview and tour if I hadn't been impressed with your written submissions. You approached stories from angles I don't know that even I would have considered. I matched the name with your face before I knew who you were. You have this electricity about you...and...well... you're beautiful."

"Thanks," she said as the alarms faded and her face cooled. "I always thought you were hot," she said before she could catch herself. "Did I just say that out loud?" He laughed.

"Yes. You did," he said and reached over to brush a piece of brown hair out of her eyelashes. "You have so much fire in you."

"Fire?" she replied laughing out loud. "I'm impulsive, bordering on stupid... Look where I am and the reason I'm here."

"You're not stupid," he said. "You're passionate."

"That's a pretty word for stupid or at least doing stupid things," she said, and they both laughed again.

"Like I said before, you have this electricity about you. You walk into a room and it becomes charged. Even if I don't see you walk in, I notice the change. I don't think I've ever felt the way I do when I'm in the same room with you," he said. "I would try to be around you only when necessary, but when I went home at night... Well, it was a reminder that I'd never felt anything remotely close to that with Emily." Alarms screamed again.

"Wait a minute," she said straightening and sobering. "Are you saying you left your wife because of me?"

"It's a little more complicated than that, but you were part of it. Even if I'm unable to have you, there was the promise of something more than what I had," he said. "Kris, I know how driven you are. You're also a lot younger than I am. No way would you give up working at the paper for an old man like me." She sat there staring at him. Her mind stormed with wine rain, and the twister of questions started to funnel down out of the clouds again. He kept his eyes on her hair. Lighting struck illuminating a question.

"How long have you been separated?" she asked quietly.

"About a year and a half," he said.

"That's only about a year after I started working there," she thought out loud.

"Yes," he said now watching her. She avoided his stare.

"But your wife and kids came to see you at your anniversary thingy, and that wasn't that long ago," she said.

"I still see my girls," he said. "I may not want to be Emily's husband anymore, but I'll always be the girls' father."

"Wow," she said as she leaned forward and put her wine glass on the coffee table in front of her. "I had no idea," she said.

"What I had with Emily wasn't much of a life, Kris," he said and pulled her back to the couch to face him. "I'm not putting pressure on you to be with me," he added. "I just want more than I had." She made herself look at him. Man, wine made him even more tempting. He was at least 20 years older than she was. He had two kids. He was her boss. There were so many strikes against him.

"I don't know what to do right now," she said.

"I understand. Want to tell me what you're thinking," he asked with a mixture of fear and hope in his voice.

"I don't think I want to say it out loud," she said.

"You can say anything to me."

"You may not like it. It may even be offensive."

"Go ahead. I can handle it."

"Could this just be one of those mid-life crisis things they're always talking about," she asked timidly. He laughed.

"I don't think so. I don't have an urge to buy a red sports car or pick up random women."

"Oh. Wouldn't you rather have a sports car than me," she

asked hopefully. "I'm really not that great. I sweat and can't cook." Had she not had so much wine, she was sure the last part would have remained just a thought. His smile never faded.

"No sports cars," he said, but the smile was losing its hold on his lips. "Are you involved with one of the Sports guys?"

"Oh! No!" she laughed and then wondered if he had seen her leave the holiday party with one of them. She decided not to mention it. "I just toy with those guys because I can, and it's fun. They're the only ones in the building who are nice to me. Since we're being honest, I kind of like the attention."

"Okay," the smile returned. She sat there quietly looking at the wine glass. "Now what's going through that amazing mind of yours?"

"You mean amazingly intoxicated, don't you? Well, I'm sure Sober Kristine would come up with a fantastically clever answer. But since she seems to have taken the night off, Drunk Kristine has mixed thoughts. Part of her wants to rip your clothes off and part of her is scared as crap and wants to run out of here," she said using her name in the third person to distance herself from the situation. "Neither of us wants to be a home wrecker, though."

"Do I get a vote," he said slyly, and they both laughed uncomfortably. "Look, Em and I weren't going to work out whether or not you came into my life. There was a time when I thought she's what I wanted. But she's too... perfect. The kids can't be kids in her house, because she's afraid they'll ruin her carpet. She spends hours trying to look perfect, make the kids look perfect, the house look perfect and put on a show for everyone. Want to know what she said when I told her I was moving out?" Kristine shrugged. This was a lot of personal information to handle at one time. "'What will our friends think?' That's what she said. Can you believe that? Not 'what about the girls?' She was worried about outside appearances. We have different priorities." Kristine felt a little uncomfortable and reached for the wine glass again.

"I think I need to sleep on this," she said. "I mean, I've always thought you were hot, and I've always had my little office fantasy about you, me and your desk, but I never thought I'd be sitting here like this," she said.

"Can I kiss you?" he asked putting his hand on her face. His hand was big and warm, and it felt like she could fall asleep with his hand on her face. This was crossing a line she wasn't sure she should. She closed her eyes and nodded tentatively. She waited in anticipation. She could feel him shifting to get a better angle. She wanted to open her eyes, but she couldn't. She felt him lift her chin and noticed how heavy she was breathing. She was a little relieved she was remembering to breathe at all. Then it happened. His lips touched hers gently at first. She returned his kiss. She started to want more, and his lips moved from hers. He kissed her cheeks and her forehead. He stood up, and she was still sitting there with her eyes closed. She slowly opened them.

"Good gravy," she whispered. He laughed out loud. He held out a hand, and she took it. He helped her to her feet, walked her around the corner and down the hall. She began to feel excitement build. He stopped outside an open door and flipped on a light within the room.

"This is your room," he said. She looked in and then looked at him confused. "Sleep on it. You've had a lot to absorb this evening. Sleep well. I promise I'll keep you safe."

"But," she said, and he gently led her into the room by placing a hand on her back and moving her toward the bed.

"I'll be across the hall," he said. "If you need anything, you know where to find me." He closed the door, and she was alone in his spare bedroom staring at the closed door. She kicked off her black heels and climbed into bed fully clothed. She grabbed her cell phone and called Derrick.

"Hello?"

"Hey. It's Kristine. What are you doing?"

"Reading Cosmo."

"Are you at work?"

"Of course. This is where I do all my reading. Slow night. No one wants to shoot anyone tonight. Are you drunk?"

"Yes."

"Are you naked in a strange man's bed?"

"No and kind of."

"Why not and who?"

"Because and Will."

"The Chief Editor guy?" he blurted, and she heard the hard binding of the magazine hit the desk or counter where Derrick sat.

"Editor-in-Chief and yes. I'm in his spare room. He's helping me with a tricky story, but he did tell me he likes me."

"So why are you in the spare room?"

"I'm thinking."

"About what? You've been hot for him for as long as I've known you."

"He's my married boss," she said.

"When was the last time you let yourself do something crazy? Buying purple lipstick that you never wear doesn't count as crazy! Use the alcohol as an excuse to get naked and jump him," Derrick said sounding more excited by the prospect than she could muster for herself.

"But that could screw up my job. Look, I'm hanging up before he wonders who I'm talking to in here," she said. She could hear Derrick yelling, "Just do it!" as she closed the phone. She rolled over.

"Sleep on it," she whispered Will's words as she drifted off to sleep.

Chapter Three

Kristine woke up with a headache and dry mouth. She looked at the big red numbers on the nightstand next to her - 7:34. She rolled on her back and rubbed her head. She didn't remember dreaming...or did she? Had the conversation with Will been a dream? She got up, dug in one of the bags for clothes and a toothbrush and set out to find the bathroom. A half hour later, she emerged from the bathroom to the smell of coffee. Her hair was still wet and hung over the white T-shirt, which was tucked into the new jeans. The T-shirt was a little snug and the jeans were a little loose - not what she would have picked out for herself. She wondered which staff member Will had sent to buy the things for her. Probably Joyce, she thought. She went into the kitchen and felt the cold tile on her bare feet. Will was standing by the toaster.

"Good morning," he said and turned around to see her. She was still fighting a hangover and confusion from last night.

"Good morning," she said and leaned back against the counter. He was staring at her and smiling. "What?"

"I don't know that I've seen you with your hair down like that. I like it," he said still grinning. She reached up and felt the cold, wet hair. "There's juice in the refrigerator and the coffee will be ready in a minute. Make yourself at home." The toast flipped up through the slits of the toaster, and Will turned his attention to buttering.

"Thanks," she said and walked to the refrigerator. It was stocked with a lot of healthy looking stuff. Her refrigerator had old mayonnaise, diet soda, a beer or two and left over Chinese take-out. She pulled out a bottle of water.

"Come on. Breakfast is served," he said and took a plate of toast and the coffee pot to the dining room. She followed him.

They sat down. "You're quiet. Not a morning person?"

"Hung over," she said and reached for a piece of toast. Will had already put some fresh fruit on the table. He poured her a cup of coffee.

"Sorry about that. I probably shouldn't have opened the second bottle." He wouldn't stop smiling. It was contagious. She smiled at him. "How did you sleep?"

"I was out as soon as my head hit the pillow," she said taking a sip of the coffee and not mentioning her conversation with Derrick. "Are you going into the office today?"

"No. I told Joyce I was working from home today. I want to help you with your story," he said. She felt a little uneasy, but she didn't know why.

"You don't have to do that," she said. "Won't people wonder what we're up to?"

"I don't care," Will said. "For the first time in my life, I don't care." She watched him. He looked happy - almost like a teenager in love for the first time. He was giddy. She wasn't sure how to react to this Will. Will was supposed to be all business. She had never thought about what he was like outside the office. "So, did you do any thinking last night?" She honestly hadn't.

"Actually, between the wine and being exhausted I think I passed out." They both sat quietly. "Will, I have to be honest. I don't know if I can take anything else right now."

"I understand," he said.

"No, please. Let me finish." He nodded. "Two months ago I was trekking along my only care in the world was how to beat everyone. Now I'm in hiding trying to crack potentially the biggest story of my life. And to top it off, this unattainable man, or so I thought, who I've been in lust with for almost three years, tells me he's separated from his wife and has feelings for me. I'm kind of overwhelmed by everything right now, but that doesn't mean no. It just means I need a little time to let all this sink in," she said.

"You're right," he said. "I shouldn't have put the added pressure on you." She smiled at him.

"It's okay, Will. It's a nice surprise. And that kiss…wow," she said blushing and looking down at the table. They both laughed. He reached across the table and put his hand on her arm.

"I'm not going anywhere," he said squeezing her arm. "Let me clear up these dishes. Want to go to the gym before we get to work?"

"Not unless The Gym is a clever name for an all you can eat dessert buffet," she said standing. "Let me help you."

"You're lucky you don't have to workout to stay in shape," he said. "Here, I'll get this. You get your stuff and take it into the office," he said. He thought she was fit, she laughed inside her head. The two flights of stairs to her apartment often left her in need of oxygen. She looked around. The condominium was bigger than she originally thought.

"Where's the office," she asked looking around the living room trying to figure out which hall to take. Will gave directions and met her in the office. She started taking notes and her computer out of the bags.

"Use my docking station," he said. She put her laptop in the docking station and pushed the button.

"Let's start at the beginning," she said. She pulled out a folder marked "disc" and opened it. She had printed the documents. "I found the news articles," she said handing three separate stacks of stapled papers to Will. "Here they are. I also have police reports, medical files - don't ask me how I got those - and some notes from people I interviewed. The one about the illegal immigrant drug dealer shooting one of his delinquent accounts is the hardest because no one wants to admit they saw anything in case this guy gets out of jail any time soon. The other two are an eight year old little boy being killed by a van that jumped the curb while he was walking to school. The van took off. Police have a description, but it didn't have license plates. The last story is about RJR Corporation acquiring a shipping company." Will flipped through the documents.

"Okay," he said. "Let me go over these and see if anything jumps out at me since I'm looking at it with fresh eyes."

"Sure. I'll work on the rest of this stack," she said and started going over the remaining documents in the folder.

Two hours later Kristine tossed her pen on the desk and rubbed her eyes. "Well, someone is cooking their books. That's all I have here."

"I've been through these four times. There has to be something here that ties them all together," he said pulling off his reading glasses.

"I need a break," she said. They went to the living room. She picked up the newspaper from the coffee table and started to scan it. Will watched her. "I'm not that interesting," she said without looking up from the paper.

"You have no idea," he said laughing. "What's wrong?" She looked puzzled.

"This woman looks familiar to me, but I don't know why," she said. She read the headline over the photo. "Wife of Robert Rawlings Leaves a Legacy of Giving." The story said Carolyn Rawlings was the wife of Robert James Rawlings, the billionaire who owned RJR Corporation along with several others. Carolyn spent her life donating her time and money to charities. She drowned in her bathtub after slipping and hitting her head. Her housekeeper found her. Kristine had a quick flash of the initials RJR. "Hold on," she said jumping up and running to the office. She brought back a stack of papers. "I know it's here somewhere," she said.

"What are you looking for?" Will asked sitting on the edge of the couch. "Let me help."

"I've got it," she said holding up one of the documents. "RJR acquired a shipping company." She looked at the photo. "Will, this is the woman who gave me the disc," she felt weak. "What if they killed her?"

"Are you sure?" He stood up and looked at the picture. He put his hand on her back to steady her as she swayed. "Sit down." She sat down and put her head between her knees. Will picked up the cordless phone sitting on the coffee table while rubbing Kristine's back with his other hand. "Joyce, get me Bronston in Business," he said. He waited a minute. "Bronston, it's Will. I want everything you have not in print on Robert James Rawlings. Email it, or give it to Joyce and have her fax it to me." There was a pause. "Yeah, thanks." Will hung up. He sat on the couch next to Kristine. She sat up, put her head in his chest and let him hold her. She suddenly, and oddly, felt safe. He kissed the top of her head. "Let's go see what else we have on him." She nodded, and they went back to the office.

They searched the paper's records and the internet to find as much as they could on Robert J. Rawlings. They found some photos. The more Kristine saw, the more positive she became Carolyn Rawlings was the woman in the street. There was a photo of Carolyn, Robert and a son named Ralston. Ralston looked to be in his early forties in the photo. About an hour into their search, the fax machine buzzed. The fax was six pages long - mostly hand written. Will read through the faxes as Kristine continued to look at the computer screen.

"Rawlings has some subsidiaries that he keeps under wraps and no one has ever been able to completely tie him to them. Some of the holdings are also overseas in some war-torn countries. Macnamar, Stormage, Carolston, Farmcorp, CRR…"

"Wait. Did you say Farmcorp?" she asked looking up at him.

"Farmcorp," he confirmed. "Why?"

"The boy's father worked for Farmcorp," she said looking through the stack of papers on the desk. "Here it is. It's on his insurance information from the hospital," she said flipping through the stapled stack. "Where are his other corporations?"

"Mostly in countries in Africa, but there's nothing specific mentioned," he said looking at the information on the fax.

"Sudan?" she asked.

"Doesn't say."

"The drug dealer was here illegally from Sudan," she said with her heart beating so hard she could feel it in her throat. "The police said he wouldn't say a word to them. They thought he didn't speak English so they brought in an interpreter, but he just didn't want to talk."

"I wouldn't talk either if I thought I was going to end up on a slab in the morgue. I'd let them put me on a plane back to Sudan and just turn around and come back," he said.

"So Robert Rawlings is our connection. Now all I have to do is fill in the holes and tie all of it together," she said excitedly.

"I don't like this," Will said apprehensively. "If this guy is willing to kill his own wife and an eight year old little boy, he wouldn't think twice about a reporter."

"Will, you have to separate the editor from the other stuff. If I was Bronston or Newman sitting here with this story, would you be so worried?"

"I'm not in love with Newman," he said sincerely and quietly. Her mouth fell open. "But, I'd still be worried. I don't want any of my reporters dying for a story. I may be a newsman, but I'm a human being first."

"You're in love with me?" she whispered, stuck on his first words. "I didn't know it was that far along. Will, you don't even know me," she said quietly. "If you knew me, I don't know that you'd feel the same way."

"Kris, I'm not a silly teenager."

"I know, but think about it. I'm a royal bitch. No one in the newsroom likes me. I'm mean to everyone, and I slept in my clothes last night," she said completely forgetting about her big story.

"You aren't a bitch, Krissy. You're defensive and you build walls around yourself. The newsroom doesn't dislike you - you just haven't given anyone a chance to get to know you," he said soothingly.

"Joyce the pit bull hates me," she said.

"She doesn't hate you. She's concerned about you."

"Concerned about me?"

"Well, I should say she's concerned about me. Joyce can read me like a book - she knows what I want before I do. She warned me away from you before I knew what was going on with me."

"Oh," she said and sat quietly for a moment. "Burt Newman hates me," she said.

"Truth be told, you're the brightest part of Burt Newman's day. Sparring with you takes his mind off the rest of his life. He thinks of you as the bratty daughter he never had," he said. She looked at him suspiciously.

"Did he tell you that?" she wondered.

"Kris, I didn't go from the mailroom to the boardroom without being able to read people," he said almost fatherly. "Give me some credit." She thought for a moment. He was good at reading people from what she could recall. "How do you think you got this job? Of course I was attracted to you immediately, but I watched you in the newsroom on your tour.

Your eyes darted around taking in everything. You asked the right questions at the right times. You had the 'it' factor I look for when I hire." She was quiet. She had no idea he watched her that closely that day. She didn't know whether to be freaked out or honored. Quick, she thought. Get off the subject. She looked down at the stack of research.

"Okay. Let's get back to my story," she said.

"Right," he said and a smile tugged at the corners of his mouth. She had no idea what she was doing. She was moving papers around. He put his hand on top of hers to stop her. "Stop. Think. What's the next step?" She thought about how he could possibly know she wasn't concentrating. Maybe he did know her.

"I need to fill the holes," she said and looked at him. "The bank records and that other weird document," she said. She pulled them out of the stack, and he looked at them over her shoulder.

"Hold on," he said. He left the room and came back with the business section of the paper. He opened to the stock pages. "See this?" He pointed to the page. "I think that's the abbreviation for RJR, and here it is on this document." She looked. He had something. He took the phone he had hooked to his waist. "Joyce, it's me. Put me through to Bronston again." Kristine wondered if Joyce knew she was staying with Will. "Are any of Rawlings' other companies public?" There was a pause. "Check it out. If they are, I want their market abbreviations. Give me whatever you find." He paced around the living room. She found him even more attractive when he took charge like that. They looked at the numbers while they waited. "If these are other companies, he's moving money around. And a lot of it," he said. "Let's go back to the office."

They went back to his home office and waited for the information. Some of the companies were public, but some weren't. Farmcorp wasn't. They matched the public companies to the abbreviations and then found one that didn't match - PMF.

"Will. PMF could be Farmcorp backwards. The P is the last letter, the F is the first and M is in the middle," she said pointing.

"If it is, he's moving a lot of money to Farmcorp," he said. "Do a search on Farmcorp." She turned to the laptop and searched in every database and search engine she could. Nothing. "We're going to spread out the research to take the focus off of you," he said. He phoned Bronston and told him to put a couple business reporters on Farmcorp. He told Bronston to tell them it was high priority but highly confidential. Their research should be done quietly. He hung up.

"What now?" she asked.

"We wait. It's going to take them awhile, but they have good contacts," he said. "Want to have some lunch?"

"Sure," she said looking for a clock. It was after 1:00. She hadn't realized so much time had passed since breakfast. Her stomach was in knots. She could feel the story beginning to unfold.

Will and Kristine made some sandwiches, and she started to relax. As Will carried the plates to the table, Kristine said, "I have a better idea." She took the plates from Will and carried them into the living room. She put the plates on the coffee table and sat on the floor. "Carpet picnic," she looked up smiling. He smiled back.

"I'll get the drinks," he said. He brought them in and put them on the glass coffee table. He sat down next to her. She shook her head.

"You can't have a carpet picnic with shoes on. Jeez! Didn't you learn anything growing up?" He took off his shoes.

She looked him over. "Better. Now, undo one or two buttons on your shirt and roll up your sleeves."

"Carpet picnics take a lot of preparation," he said as he did what she asked. She watched carefully.

"I think that's it," she said and reached for her sandwich. "We used to have carpet picnics growing up," she said before taking a bite of her turkey sandwich.

"Ah," he said and started eating his sandwich.

"We also used to make forts out of furniture," she said.

"Forts? How did you do that?"

"Oh come on," she said. "Forts. You know with sheets or blankets and furniture." He laughed. "Seriously," she added.

"Sounds like fun."

"You've never made forts? Not even for the girls?" she asked in disbelief.

"Can't say as I have. Plus, the girls' mother wouldn't exactly allow us to make a mess of her furniture." Kristine looked around and found a throw blanket on a chair. She stood up and unfolded the blanket. She put one corner on the mantle of the fireplace and weighed it down with a heavy candlestick. She took the other corner to the other end of the mantle and put a leaded glass vase on that corner. She walked over to the glass coffee table. Will watched her in amusement.

"Look out," she said. He moved a bit and she slid the glass table closer to the fireplace. She took the other ends of the blanket and found weights for them. She placed the ends of the blanket on the opposite ends of the coffee table. "Come on in to Fort Kris," she said and went under the blanket. He followed her, and they sat on the hearth while they finished their lunch. Will couldn't stop smiling. "See? Isn't this fun? I don't think I've ever had a fort with a fireplace, though. This is a fancy fort."

"You're amazing," he said looking at her. She smiled. She

didn't think she had ever been called amazing and didn't really see anything amazing about a carpet picnic or a fort.

"Eh, you're just saying that because you're in my fort."

"No, you're truly amazing," he said.

"Thanks. I don't think I've ever been amazing to anyone before today," she said quietly.

"That's not true," he said and took her hand. "You have a gift." She looked at her hand in his. His hand was so big it swallowed hers.

"I think I should warn you I'm not very good at relationship stuff," she edged closer to him. He leaned into her.

"Neither am I. Maybe we can learn together." His voice was deep and soothing.

"This is totally unexpected," she said smiling. "But, I think I want to see where this goes." His smile grew wider. He leaned in to kiss her.

"You've made me a happy man," he said and kissed her again.

"Will this impact my job?" she asked nervously wondering if she had made the correct decision. He sighed, and she thought she knew the answer.

"It should, but not right now. We'll take things slow and deal with office policy when we have to."

"Won't you get into trouble if the publisher finds out?"

"Let me deal with it when the time comes," he added. "For now, we're just getting to know each other better. No harm in that." She smiled weakly.

They spent the rest of the day in the fort. She told him about her childhood, and he told her about his. They talked about politics, religion and world affairs. She couldn't remember a time when she had been more open with anyone, especially a man. Of course, most of the men she dated couldn't name three current events other than who won what sporting event. She had a huge story waiting for her, she thought. It will be there in the morning. They laughed at each other's silly jokes.

After a late dinner, they spent the evening snuggling on the couch. She must have fallen asleep in his arms, because he woke her with a kiss to the forehead. "Time for bed, sleepy head," he said. They walked down the hall hand-in-hand and stopped at the bedroom doors. She turned to him.

"I think I should sleep in here," she said nodding to the spare bedroom.

"Yeah," he said disappointed. "I'm still technically a married man." She nodded. They kissed goodnight and parted in the hall.

Chapter Four

Between the budding relationship with her boss and the story she wanted finished, Kristine couldn't sleep. She got up, went to the kitchen, got a bottle of water and headed back to the office. She did another search on Robert Rawlings. There were a lot of hits. No, there were a ton of hits. She sighed and started going through each one.

There's no way to know how much time passed before she opened the story about the reopening of an RJR manufacturing plant only days after a tornado nearly destroyed it. There were photos, which she clicked through one by one. The President of the United States was visiting to congratulate the workers for getting the plant going so quickly. There were different shots of the president shaking hands with Rawlings behind a production line. Something caught her eye. She clicked on the zoom button. She clicked again and again. Her heart leapt into her throat. The Sudanese drug dealer was standing in the background! "Oh my God," she whispered. She pushed the print button, but she wasn't mapped to print to Will's printer. She ran to his room and burst through the door without knocking. "It's him!"

"What?" Will asked groggily looking at the clock. It was 3:15 a.m.

"Will, you have to see this," she tugged at his arm.

"Okay, okay," he said as he got out of bed. Will was only wearing silk boxer shorts, so he grabbed a robe on his way out of his room. She led him back to the office and pointed to the screen.

"The drug dealer who shot that guy," she said. She had the photo blown up so much you couldn't see the rest of it. "That's him and it's Rawlings."

"Slow down," Will said still waking up. She looked at the screen, but it was grainy.

"Hold on," she said and clicked back through to make the photo smaller. Will looked closely.

"Let me see the mug shot," he said. She pulled out the photo and put it next to the computer screen. "Blow it up again." She did that, too. "I'll be damned," he said as he leaned toward the screen.

"The photo didn't run anywhere. I found it in the AP archives. He's not in any of the other ones I've seen," she said excitedly. "Do you think there's some sort of connection to the White House? Do you? Because I'm not afraid to go there," she said at a high rate of speed.

"Whoa. Just because he was there at the opening, I don't think you can lump him into anything," Will said. "Send a request to the AP for the photo. We'll run it with the story. Not now though. I don't want anyone seeing the time on the request. It will set off bells if someone sees you working at 3:15 in the morning."

"Okay," she was bubbling inside. "Will, this is it. I now have all the stories tied to Rawlings. This is a huge piece."

"I agree, but it's almost 3:30. Let's go back to bed and tackle this in the morning," he said.

"But," she said in protest.

"But nothing. I'm still your boss, and that's an order," he took her hand. "Come on." She reluctantly left the office and went back to bed.

* * * * *

Will knocked on Kristine's door around 7 o'clock. "Yeah," she grumbled. He walked in and went to the side of her bed. She was sleeping on her stomach. She shifted up onto her elbows. "Mmm.. You smell good," she said sleepily. "What's up?" He sat on the edge of her bed. He was in a suit.

"I'm going into the office for a little while this morning," he said playing with her hair. She rolled on her side and brushed a piece of lint off his suit leg.

"Do you have to?"

"I have to sign some papers and take care of some business. I'll be home by lunch," he said. "Just make yourself at home and don't do anything impulsive before I get back." He stood up.

"Promise," she said. He kissed her forehead and started to leave.

"Be back soon. Go back to sleep," he said as he closed the door.

* * * * *

Kristine was showered, dressed and in the office when Will returned. He brought lunch with him.

"Kris, I'm home," he called from the kitchen. He was getting dishes and opening boxes when she came into the kitchen and hugged him from behind.

"How was your day, dear?" she asked in a *Leave it to Beaver* tone. He turned around abruptly and looked at her. "What?"

"Nothing. It's nothing," he said.

"No, tell me," she said poking him in the side and taking a step backwards. He turned and said.

"It just brought back a memory, that's all," he said.

"Oh," she said only slightly understanding.

"I heard that same phrase every day for 16 years," he said. Her heart sunk.

"Oh," she said again. "I'm sorry."

"Hey, hey," he said as he walked to her and took her in his arms. "No, I'm sorry. Things like that are bound to happen when you've been with someone for so long." He kissed the top of her head. "Want some lunch?"

"Yeah, I'm hungry," she said leaning back to look up at him. "What was up at the office?" She chose her words carefully so they were safe.

"I met with Bronston," he said turning to finish putting the food on plates. "He didn't have much, but he said there are some rumors that Rawlings has a lot of interest in Sudan."

"Interesting," she said following him into the dining room. He paused and continued into the living room. She smiled to herself. They sat in front of the coffee table. "No one will go on record if they feel their life is threatened, so I'm going to have to find another source. I wonder if that's what happened to the eight year old."

"Mmm," he said swallowing. "Maybe. I want to bring in the authorities on this. Unless we get enough for an indictment, you'll be in danger," he said. "I did some checking today to see who we can trust, and our legal options."

"I don't know. That sounds like a big gamble. What if they ice my story?"

"We'll figure out something," he said and took a drink of bottled water. "I also had another meeting," he said looking at her to see her reaction. She raised her eyebrows. "I met with a divorce attorney." The eyebrows went higher and her eyes bulged.

"Really?" she replied. "Why now?"

"I wasn't as motivated as I am now," he said. She sighed heavily and shook her head.

"I don't want to be the reason for all this," she said tossing her sandwich on her plate. "Sixteen years is a long time."

"You aren't the reason," he said and put his hand on her

leg. "You're the sunlight at the end of a very long tunnel."

"Well, that's a lot of pressure. Heating and lighting the earth, jeez!" she laughed. He squeezed her leg.

They used the rest of the afternoon and evening to make phone calls, search for more information on Rawlings and finally went to their individual beds after midnight. The phone rang a little after 4 a.m. Kristine rolled over. Ten minutes later Will came into her room.

"Kris?"

"What's going on?" She rolled over to face him. The light outlined his frame in a silhouette.

"Honey, that was the police. They're on their way here," he said. "I want you to stay back here. I'm going to pack up your stuff and put it in here with you."

"What's wrong?"

"They found Bronston. He's dead," he said as his voice trailed.

"What?!" she sat up in the bed.

"He was found in a park shot to death," he said.

"Oh my God," she whispered in disbelief. "Did we do this?"

"No. Now let me get your stuff and make sure there's no sign of you here."

"What are you going to tell them?"

"I'm not sure, but I will protect you," he said.

"Will, what if they come after you?" she asked growing more and more upset and frightened.

"I'll be fine," he replied. "Now let me get your things." She got out of bed and helped him. They put her belongings in the closet. She made the spare bed and put her bags in the closet. "I'm going to leave the door open to avoid suspicion." She nodded.

"Be careful," she said and climbed in the closet with her

53

bags. She sat down and leaned against the wall to be as comfortable as she could. She didn't know how long she would be there. He backed out of the room and smoothed the footprints as he went. If anyone walked down the hall, there would be no trail leading into the second bedroom or near the closet.

The door buzzed at 4:45 a.m. Will let the police into the penthouse. Kristine couldn't hear what anyone said, and she stayed as still as she could in the closet. She wasn't sure how much time had passed, but it seemed like hours before she heard someone come into the spare bedroom. The door opened and the light hurt her eyes.

"I'm sorry," Will said as he reached down to help her out of the closet. "I didn't think they would ever leave."

"What did they say?" she asked stretching.

"Nothing really. They just asked a lot of questions about Bronston, whether he had any enemies and what he had been working on. They want to go through his desk and some back issues of the paper. I'm going to meet them at the office in a couple of hours. Come here," he said and turned her around to rub her shoulders. It felt so good she let her head drop forward.

"What did you tell them," she asked feeling the magic of his fingers on her skin and over the straps of her white tank top, working her muscles.

"The truth. I told them about how I had asked him to get some information on RJR Corporation. I'm going to stop by his apartment to see if there's anything I can do for his family when I leave the paper. I may be home late."

"Sure. Do whatever you need to do," she said. "I think I'm going to work on the story today. I may start writing it and just fill in the blanks later." He stopped rubbing her shoulders and pulled her into him.

"I don't think I have to tell you how important it is for you to be careful," he said softly. She nodded. She turned in his arms to face him.

"You look so tired," she whispered. Her heart hurt at the thought she was the reason he lost sleep. "Can you go back to bed for a while? I'll hold you while you sleep or you can hold me." He was quiet for a minute.

"I wish I could, but I have to get to the office," he said in a disappointed tone. "I need to be there on a day like today."

"You're right," she said. He was gone within 45 minutes, and she sat in front of her computer screen. It was blank. She put her fingers on the keys. Bronston Marshall ran through her mind. She didn't know him. He worked in a different section of the paper on a different floor. Now he was dead because he was helping get details for her story. She wondered if Will felt any guilt for asking him to get the information. What if Will became a target? She felt a tear roll down her cheek. She was going to do the rest of this on her own. She opened her email. There was a message in there from a law firm. She opened it. It was from Carolyn Rawlings' lawyer. He said he had something Carolyn wanted her to have in case of her death, and he had to give it to her in person. She hit the reply button and typed the words, "Meet me in the emergency room of County General Hospital at noon." She figured the hospital would have many different entrances and exits, be crowded and would be a good place to be if she got shot.

She sent the email. She sifted through papers organized neatly on Will's desk looking for something with his address on it. She found an electric bill then checked to see if Will lived on a bus line. She wrote down a bus number, packed her computer and files into her bag and went to her bedroom. She packed one bag with what she thought she would need for a day or two. She took the money Will had gotten the day they left the office together. She also took her cell phone and the cell phone registered to the paper. She put her bags on the chair in the living room and then wrote Will a note. It said:

> Will,
>   As long as you're helping me, you're in danger. I couldn't live with myself if anything happened to you. I'll call you tonight.

She hesitated for a moment before she signed it. Should she just sign her name or should she put the word love before it? If she did, should she spell it l-o-v-e or l-u-v? She settled on drawing a heart and put a K under it. She put the note on the kitchen counter where he would find it.

The bus would pick her up a block away, and she had 15 minutes to get there. She took a deep breath and left the safety of the penthouse.

Chapter Five

She took the bus to the subway and the subway back into the heart of the city. She found a hotel and got in line to check in. There was a young man and a young woman working behind the counter. She hoped to be lucky enough to get the young man to help her, and she did. She walked up to the counter. The young man, whose name tag said Brady, smiled and said, "How can I help you?"

"I'd like a non-smoking room please," she said hoisting her bags on her shoulder. They were heavy, but she was afraid to put them on the ground.

"King or two doubles?" he asked looking in the computer.

"Whatever is available," she said. She reached in her pocket for money while he clicked through the computer.

"Okay," he said. "I'll need a credit card."

"Oh great," she said flustered. "This has been the worst day of my life!" She made her lip quiver as though she was going to cry. Brady looked helplessly at her. "I no sooner got into town and someone picked my pocket," she sniffed at the end of the sentence.

"That sucks," he said. She nodded and pretended to wipe away a tear.

"They got my credit card and my ID," she said. "Luckily, I had most of my cash stashed in one of my other bags. I only need the hotel for a couple of nights until my friend gets back into town. I'm staying with her, but she had to stay a couple of days later than she thought on her assignment. I didn't want to change all my plans so I thought I'd just get a hotel until she gets back. She's modeling in Paris right now." Brady's eyes widened. "Do you think I could just pay cash?" she asked sweetly.

"Um, I'm really not supposed to," he said looking around.

"Oh please. If you don't help me, I'll have to sleep on the streets until my friend gets home," she said lip quivering again.

"Oh, okay," he said looking around nervously. "I'll figure out how to trick the system. We comp people sometimes."

"Comp people?" she asked knowing the answer.

"Yeah, people can stay for free if the management says it is okay."

"Are you good with computers?" she flirted.

"Yeah, it's my major," he said clicking away. He handed her a room key and took the money for a two night stay. She wasn't sure if the money would end up going in the drawer or helping to pay for Brady's college education. Either way, she didn't care as long as she had a place to stay.

She went to her room. She had an hour before she had to meet the man claiming to be Carolyn Rawlings' attorney. She thought it would be a good idea to get to the hospital early.

She entered through the main hospital entrance and walked the halls to the emergency room. She snuck back into the admitting area and found someone she knew. Kristine wasn't sure it was a good or bad thing that through her years of reporting she knew most of the people working in the city's emergency rooms.

Derrick loved to talk to Kristine and see himself in the paper even if he was an unnamed source. He also liked to talk about shoes, purses, cute Hollywood actors and makeup. Derrick's outward appearance was phenomenal - masculine and pretty at the same time. He was about Kristine's height, and he lifted weights regularly. His skin was the color of creamy coffee and as smooth as glass. He had black hair and black eyes with eyelashes that reached all the way to his well-groomed eyebrows. Derrick had wanted to be a doctor, but that's an expensive and time consuming education.

Like most other hospitals, County General Hospital's emergency room wasn't a happy place. Shootings, overdoses and the bizarre were common nearly every minute of every day. Today was no different. Kristine caught Derrick's attention and motioned him behind an empty curtain.

"Hey, girlfriend," he said and gave her a kiss on each cheek. "You look like someone they usually roll in here on a gurney," he said.

"That's actually not funny," she said, and his look took a turn for the serious.

"What happened with Chief Running News guy?"

"Not much. I'm working a really big story."

"I've been trying to call you," he said. "There was a huge shoe sale yesterday!"

"I haven't had my cell on since we talked the last time," she said. "Look, I need your help."

"Sure. What do you want me to do?" he asked always eager to be part of the action.

"I'm supposed to meet someone in the waiting room at noon," she said. "I need you to scope it out for me - make sure he looks okay - and then I may need your help getting out of here so no one can follow me."

"Girlfriend, what are you into?" he asked worried.

"It's just a big story," she said. "I'll be fine once it runs." Or at least she hoped. "Anyway, this guy should be carrying an envelope or disc or something."

"I'll keep an eye out on the waiting area," Derrick said. "Come on, I'll get you something to wear so you'll fit in back here." Derrick gave Kristine the top portion of scrubs and put her in the staff lounge. She took off the denim jacket she was wearing and put the scrubs on over her white T-shirt. "Wait here." He obviously loved being involved in a story. He opened the door to the lounge, looked suspiciously up and down the hall, turned to her and gave the thumbs up and walked out. She smiled and shook her head.

Shortly after noon, Derrick came bursting through the staff lounge door. "Come on," he yelled. This wasn't exactly the quiet exchange she had planned.

"What is it?" Kristine asked, standing.

"They just brought in a guy who was in a hit and run right outside. I think he tried to say your name before they intubated him." Derrick turned and took off at a fast pace with Kristine following closely. Chaos surrounded the gurney where a tiny man in brown dress pants and yellow dress shirt fought for his life. One leg was bent half way down his shin. Blood soaked the gurney. Derrick led Kristine to the head of the gurney. "This is Kristine," he said. The man's eyes, full of fear, darted to her. He began to grunt and point to a suit jacket hanging on the wall. It matched the brown pants.

"Who did this to you?" she asked breathing hard and knowing the answer. He grunted louder and pointed to the jacket again, more urgency in his eyes.

"You want this?" Derrick asked walking to wall.

"What the hell is going on," one of the doctors said.

"I'm helping a patient. I suggest you do the same and worry about him, not me," Derrick said in his bitchiest of tones. Had Kristine not been so scared, she would have laughed out loud. Derrick pulled an envelope from the inside jacket pocket. The man's head nodded, and he lost consciousness. "Let's go," Derrick said and grabbed Kristine by the arm.

They left the emergency room, ran down a stairwell and out of the hospital into the employee garage. Derrick handed Kristine the envelope and said, "Go, and be careful, gorgeous." He gave her a kiss on the cheek and went back into the hospital. She opened the envelope, took out the contents, which was a sheet of paper and a disc. She folded the paper and put it in her mouth. She pulled the scrubs over her head and untucked her T-shirt and stuck both the disc and the paper into her jeans. She left the shirt untucked. She threw the envelope in the garbage can by the door and made her way through the garage and toward sunlight. She got on the first bus she saw and didn't pay attention to where it was going. Three stops later, when she saw a large crowd exiting, she decided to blend in with them. She got off the bus and followed the crowd to the subway. She found a subway going back toward her hotel, but she decided to take more than one. Kristine tried not to look nervous as her eyes scanned the faces to see if anyone was following her.

She made it back to her hotel room and called the police station nearest the hospital. One of her sources told her witnesses at the hit and run said the car's passenger got out of the car and took Carolyn Rawlings' lawyer's briefcase. Amazing, she thought. She called the hospital and found out the lawyer was in critical condition. She put the disc into her laptop and opened the paper.

> Ms. Larkin,
>
> My name is Carolyn Rawlings, and if you're reading this, I'm dead. I was the woman who bumped into you on the street and put the disc in your bag. I don't know if you're investigating the story, but I haven't seen your byline lately.
>
> I have more information on this disc. It will help you tie together the pieces of the last disc. I didn't give this to you the first time, because my husband would have known someone close

to the family gave it to you. I had to protect my
son and his family.

Be safe.

CR

Kristine felt a lump in her throat and swallowed hard. She
spent the next seven hours reading over the files on the disc
and writing her story. Robert Rawlings was a business man
with a lot of secrets. He used his companies as fronts to run
drugs and sell arms. What Kristine couldn't understand is the
"I had to protect my son and his family" line in Carolyn
Rawlings' letter. As far as Kristine could tell, the information
on the disc implicated her son Ralston as being her husband's
protégé, and Ralston Rawlings didn't have a wife and kids.

She filed her story, emailed a copy to Will for insurance
and put all her documentation in her bag. She had to put it
someplace safe, because she would need it if someone ever
questioned her reporting or the facts of the story. She realized
she had forgotten to call Will and wondered why he hadn't
called her. Her heart sank. What if something had happened
to him? She found the paper's cell phone. She had turned it
off after calling the hospital and police station. It was late, but
she decided to call him anyway. The phone rang once.

"Kristine?" The voice sounded frantic.

"Yeah, Will. It's me," she said and heard him breathe a
sigh of relief.

"Thank God. I've been so worried about you. Did you
hear about Carolyn Rawlings' lawyer?"

"Yeah, I did. It's unbelievable," she said. She debated
telling him she had been there, but she wasn't sure who else
may be listening. "I put it to bed," she said knowing he would
know the newspaper jargon.

"Already?" he replied.

62

"Yes. It was time," she said.

"Where are you? No, wait. Don't tell me," he said. "Can you come home?" She wondered for a minute what he meant by "home." She didn't want to go into that on the phone and wondered if she had been on the line too long.

"I'll call you this afternoon," she said and flipped the phone closed. She knew the story wouldn't run in the morning paper for two reasons - she submitted it too late, and the lawyers would have to review it. Still, she felt a sense of relief to have it into the metro editor's desk.

She woke to a cell phone ringing. She looked at the clock. It was 7:30 in the morning.

"Hello?" she said in her morning voice.

"Ms. Larkin, I'd liked to speak to you privately," a man's voice said. She jolted awake and thought for a moment.

"I'd like to win the lottery. It's nice to have a dream."

"This is a serious matter," he said.

"And you are?" she asked suspiciously.

"I'll tell you everything when we meet," he said. She sat up in the bed.

"You know, I'm pretty booked, but if you have your people call my people, maybe we can work out something oh say…in the next 6 months or so," she said sarcastically.

"This is no joking matter. You are in a lot of danger," he said.

"No kidding? Wow. Well, then I'll definitely go meet you, a strange man who won't identify himself. How about we meet in a dark alley where no one will see us?" she replied, growing in sarcasm.

"Okay, I see you aren't going to make this easy," he said. "I'm a federal agent. I'd like to meet you in 20 minutes at your favorite coffee shop." She thought about it for a minute.

"No. If I decide to meet you, it will be on my terms," she

said.

"Ms. Larkin, you are seriously jeopardizing my life as well as your own," he said.

"You must think I'm crazier than you are if you think I'm going to trust you no questions asked," she said.

"You're still alive because of me."

"And what about Bronston Marshall and Carolyn Rawlings? Do they have you to thank for keeping them alive, too? Oh wait, they're dead."

"I'm sorry about them, but you have been my primary responsibility," he replied.

"You're going to have to give me more than that if you want me to meet you," she said conscious of the time she was spending on the call. She'd be leaving the hotel soon. He paused.

"My name is Justin McMichaels. I'm undercover working in the RJR Corporation. Call the FBI offices - they'll verify it. I'll give them a public meeting place and time for them to give you," he said. "I'm taking a huge risk with you," he said and disconnected.

She called the FBI offices and asked to speak to Justin McMichaels. She was connected to a woman.

"Eileen Masters," she said.

"I'm looking for a Justin McMichaels," Kristine replied.

"Ah, yes. Justin just informed me you would be calling Ms. Larkin," Eileen Masters said. "I must say, he's taking a great risk identifying himself to you."

"Well, that's awfully nice of him. You see, I have a little bit of a problem meeting some strange man whenever and wherever he tells me. I guess you could say he had to identify himself, or he'd be very lonely at our meeting," she said.

"That's good. You shouldn't trust anyone," she said. "Still, my first priority is to my agents."

"My first priority is me - hope you understand," Kristine said.

"Of course," Eileen said. "McMichaels has been working this case for years."

"If you ask me, he isn't very good. He should have come to me. I've gotten quite a bit on Rawlings in just a few months," she said bragging a little.

"So I hear. That's not necessarily a good thing for you Ms. Larkin," Eileen said. "Now, McMichaels would like to meet you at 1:00 at Italianos. Do you know where that is?"

"Yes."

"And bring the information you have," she said. Right, Kristine thought. Like there was a chance in hell she would hand over that information before her story ran in the paper. They disconnected.

Kristine showered quickly and packed the few things she had out of the bags. She left the hotel down the stairwell. She spent the next several hours traveling through the city switching between buses and subways. She found a post office and picked out some mailing materials so she could mail the discs and other material to the paper. She debated for a minute as to whose name to put on them. Will's may be too obvious so she picked Joyce's name. They would still make it to Will. She stood in line and sent off the discs and notes certified mail.

At 12:30, she finally started weaving her way through the city to the restaurant. She realized she wouldn't recognize Justin McMichaels. She entered the restaurant cautiously. The hostess asked if she could help her. It was very crowded and people were waiting for tables. There was a bar toward the back of the room on the right. The left side went farther back, and the kitchen was behind the mirrored back wall of the bar.

"I'm supposed to be meeting someone," Kristine said looking around. She was five minutes late.

"Follow me," the hostess said and turned to walk toward the back of the room. Kristine followed nervously. There was a table across from the bar and the kitchen entrance where a man in a black suit sat. He didn't look like a man named Justin McMichaels. He looked like a man named Bob or Ed. "Here you go. Can I take your bags for you?"

"No," she said abruptly. "Thank you." McMichaels stood and reached out a hand to Kristine. She shook it.

"Nice to meet you, Ms. Larkin," he said. He sat down facing the front door, which left the seat across from him open. Kristine didn't like sitting with her back to the door so she slid the chair to the right a little. Her back was to the bar now. She put her bags on the floor next to her. "I'm Agent McMichaels."

"Hi," she said nervously looking around.

"You're safe here. This place is full of federal agents," he said reaching for the bread basket. He offered her some first. She shook her head no, and he took a piece. She unconsciously hugged her menu to her chest for security and looked around the restaurant. McMichaels was average in almost every way. He was average height. He was average build. The only distinguishing feature was a slightly receding hair line and a bald patch on the top of his head toward the back of his scalp. He wore a blue tie and a white shirt. "Did you bring the information?" he asked buttering his bread.

"The information is safe," she said. She couldn't help but look from face to face trying to figure out who was a Fed and who wasn't.

"I don't think it's going to come as a surprise to you that Rawlings knows you're working on a story," he said. She shook her head again. She had an uneasy feeling about this meeting. "We think Mr. Rawlings is responsible for the sudden death of his wife."

"Shocking," she quietly blurted out. The restaurant was loud enough she was sure no one could overhear their conversation.

"We have reason to believe that Carolyn Rawlings tried to get information to you via her lawyer," he said.

"Really? What makes you say that?" she asked innocently.

"We have an eyewitness that puts you in the emergency room, and we have video surveillance from the hospital indicating you left with an envelope."

"I can honestly say I didn't leave the hospital property with an envelope," she said.

"Your nurse friend hasn't been cooperating with us either," he added. "We've had him at headquarters since yesterday."

"There's a difference between not cooperating and not knowing anything. Derrick is a great guy who wants to help me, but he doesn't know a thing about what's going on with my story. I made sure of that so people like you wouldn't have anything on him. I'd recommend you let him go, or there will be an added side bar to my piece naming you as a Fed," she said putting the menu on the table feeling as though she had regained some power. He smiled and nodded his head.

"You're young, but you're shrewd," he said.

"Young doesn't always mean stupid," she said reaching across the table and taking a piece of bread from the basket, although she still felt sick to her stomach with nerves.

"You can have your story," he said.

"Damn straight," she said.

"But, we want the information you were given," he said. "It is part of a criminal investigation."

"You have it," she said. "Or at least the government has it right now."

"Care to elaborate?" he asked.

"Not really. Not until I walk out of here alive, and I know

Derrick is released."

"You seem to think you're running this show," he said. She could feel him getting frustrated. This meeting obviously wasn't what he had anticipated.

"I don't understand something," she said. "Why would you blow your cover when you could have had some other Fed approach me?" He sat quietly looking at her. "I mean, that's a big risk if these people are so dangerous and you've spent years of your life on this case." She raised her eyebrows. "Isn't it?" A smile crept at the corner of his mouth.

"Young and pretty smart," he replied. Just as he started another sentence his attention was drawn to the front door. "Go!" he yelled to her and jumped up out of his seat, gun drawn. Before she knew what was happening there was gunfire from all directions. People were screaming, glass was breaking, and her chair tipped. She fell onto the floor and scurried toward the bar. She huddled behind the bar. She saw a flash beside her. The bartender, a young man, dressed in black pants, black shoes and a white shirt had pulled a gun from behind the bar and fired over the top of the bar. Bottles shattered on the wall above her raining glass and liquor. She covered her head with her hands. The young man fell on the floor next to her. She wasn't sure how long the gunfire lasted, but it felt like it was hours, maybe days, maybe months.

Just as she was thinking about making a run out through the kitchen, the gunfire started to subside. She was afraid to look over or around the bar. Soon, there was quiet. She heard a voice and fought the urge to yell for help. "Make sure we got them all and find the bag," the voice said. She realized she was in more trouble. She heard a single gunshot. She didn't know what was happening, but she imagined they were finishing off anyone with a little life left in them. She crawled quickly over broken glass to the body lying on the floor next to her. The noises she made were covered by moans, gunshots and other crunching coming from the restaurant.

She put her finger in the pool of blood and drew a line of blood from the corner of her mouth to her chin. She quickly positioned herself so she was sharing the pool of blood with the bartender. Not typically a religious woman, she said a quick prayer and apologized to God for being a stranger. There must have been three more shots before one of the men made it back to the bar area. She held her breath and kept her eyes open and still. He nudged her with his foot, but she didn't move. There were sounds of sirens in the background.

"Let's get out of here," the man's voice called. He looked right at her and smiled - proud of himself that she was dead, she thought. His face was burned into her memory - she recognized him as Ralston Rawlings. She thought she counted three men leave through the kitchen, and one was carrying her bags. She started to panic and shake. She turned her head and looked into eyes of the bartender, which didn't show signs of life. A mixture of blood and booze soaked her hair, clothes, skin. The smell overtook the garlic of the Italian food. She scurried away from the body next to her, leaned up against the back of the bar, pulled her knees to her chest and began to cry. That's the last thing she remembered clearly. Despite her best efforts, Kristine Larkin died that day.

Chapter Six

What happened next was a blur. She remembered bits and pieces. She remembered the bright lights at the hospital, and someone picking glass out of her legs, arms and hands. She remembered blurry faces asking her question after question. She asked for her mom. She asked for her dad. She asked for Will. She asked for Derrick. She thought she may have even asked for Burt Newman. No one came. She thought she spent a couple of days in the hospital, but she wasn't sure.

Somehow she was transported from the hospital to a house. The shades were always drawn, and there were always at least two people with guns in the room with her or right outside the door. The doctors said she was in shock, or at least she thought she heard them say that. She was at the house for about a week and a half before she could even have an intelligent conversation with anyone.

She was at the kitchen table one morning when she realized she hadn't seen a newspaper since the morning of the shooting. She looked up at the woman sitting next to her. Megan Rice spoke in a complete sentence for the first time. "I'd like a newspaper," she said, her voice cracking.

"I'll have to see if that's allowed," the woman said very dryly. She looked at the woman noticing her features. Everything seemed to be new.

"Who are you?" she asked. "Where am I? What's happening?"

"You know who I am, Megan," the woman said impatiently. "I've been with you since the hospital." Megan looked confused.

"My name isn't Megan. It's Kristine," she said.

"Not anymore."

"I don't understand," she said. Her mind was fuzzy. She looked at her bandaged hands.

"That's the shock and pain killers wearing off," the woman said.

"Who are you?" Megan asked again.

"I'm Eileen Masters," she said. Megan remembered having a conversation with someone named Eileen Masters the day of the shooting.

"Why am I here?"

"You're testifying that Ralston Rawlings shot a bunch of federal agents," she said. "I figured you owed us that much. You'll be here long enough for us to get your testimony submitted, and then you'll be given a new place to live and a new job."

"I don't understand," she said. "I want to talk to Will Montgomery."

"I'm sure you do. I want to talk to Justin McMichaels. I'm sure his family would like that, too." Megan thought about that statement for a moment.

"Did he die?"

"Yes, he did. So did five other agents in the restaurant along with 12 civilians." Megan choked on the words she heard.

"Oh my God," she whispered. "I'm so sorry."

"Your little game got out of hand, didn't it?" Eileen Masters didn't like Kristine or Megan or whatever her name was now. "There are some of us who put our lives on the line every day trying to make this a better world to live in for people who aren't worth it." Megan knew this meant her by the tone of the woman's voice. "A lot of them died that day trying to protect you. And you... You had no regard for anyone other than yourself, you stupid girl."

"Eileen," a male's voice said as he walked into the kitchen.

"That's enough." Megan recognized the guy. He had been in the house with them.

"Is Will Montgomery okay?" she asked the man.

"Yes. He's fine. He didn't take the news of your death very well, though." Megan felt herself start crying and breathing hard.

"Will thinks I'm dead?" she replied.

"Everyone does. The story of your untimely demise ran right next to your story about Rawlings," Eileen said.

"My mom and dad think I'm dead, too?" she asked not fully comprehending what she heard.

"Everyone and most importantly the bad guys," the man said.

"How can I testify if I'm dead?" she wondered out loud hoping to get some sort of opening to reclaim her name and her life.

"You identified the man responsible for the shooting before you died in the hospital," the man said. "We just have to make sure we get everything taken care of so there are no legal loopholes."

Megan stood up and walked to her bedroom. She wondered what she had done. Everything and everyone she loved was gone. She wondered if they mourned her. Would Will go back to Emily? She wished he could go with her wherever she was going. She didn't want to be alone. She knew she couldn't do that to him, though. He still had two little girls who needed him, and he needed them. Part of her wished she really had died in that horrible restaurant. The noise of the guns popped in her head. The smell of the garlic and alcohol overtook her senses. She began to cry harder. Think of something happy. She thought of the first dinner she had with Will in his apartment. The wine, the Italian food - no, not Italian food. She put her hands on her head. She forced the memory of their carpet picnic into her mind. Will's smile and delight at the fort almost made her smile. She couldn't go back there. She couldn't go back to the comfort of her parents' house and her old room. She couldn't sit outside a café on a Sunday and talk with Derrick about who was cheating on whom in Hollywood. She let out a small moan and rolled onto her side. She hugged her knees up to her chest and cried herself to sleep.

Chapter Seven

Megan Rice was a shell. She woke up in the morning, she went to her job teaching English to high school kids, and she went home. Her home was a one bedroom apartment on the third floor of a no frills three-story red brick building. She hadn't bothered to collect many things. She had a sofa, a side table, a television and a treadmill in the living room. The dining room had a table with a computer on it and a single chair. Her bedroom had a bed, nightstand and a chest of drawers. Her long, beautiful brown hair was now shoulder length and blonde. Her once stylish clothes that fit in so well in New York were replaced by mid-west casual wear. She didn't smile much. She talked at school in class when she had to teach. She had no friends. She had no joy. She had no life.

Megan turned toward the class, who stared at her. She wondered how long she had been looking at the board. She cleared her throat. "I know we have a long weekend, and you really don't want any homework." The faces had a look of anticipation. She had intended to add a "but" to that sentence and hand out a writing assignment. She took a deep breath. "So, enjoy it. Do something you've always wanted to do - as long as it's legal - and I'll ask you to write something when you get back." The bell sounded, and she added, "Have fun." The kids crowded out of the room, and she sat down at her desk. She opened her desk and took out a stack of papers from a spelling test earlier in the day. She was probably the only teacher in the school that gave students their papers graded with comments the day after they handed them in to her. The words on the first test started to run together. That's it, she thought. "I have to get out of here," she said. She put the tests in her bag, got out her purse and locked her desk.

The drive home was only 15 minutes. She was packed and back in her car in 20 minutes. She wasn't sure where she was going, and she wasn't even sure she was coming back. At the airport, she parked in the long-term lot and caught a shuttle to the terminals. She chose an airline at random and walked to the desk.

"I need a ticket for a plane leaving within the next half hour," she said to the agent. The agent looked puzzled. Megan thought about what she was asking, and it sounded crazy even to her. "I just need to get away for a little while."

"I understand," the clerk said with a comforting smile as if she knew exactly what plagued the young woman. Megan rolled her eyes to herself. How nice it would be to want to get away for a weekend because the kids were driving her crazy, or an argument with a boyfriend or just a rash, PMS-induced decision. The clerk tapped keys on the keyboard. Not hard like Burt Newman, but more quietly as Kristine used to do. She found a flight landing near a winter resort in New York. "It's very quaint. My husband took me there for our anniversary a few years back. You can make New York in a day if you decide to go into the city," she added. "There's a shuttle to the resorts when you get off the plane." Megan stood motionless for a moment. Was it crazy to go so close to those she knew? She knew she shouldn't, but the temptation to be closer to Will was too much for her. Who looked for a dead woman, anyway? "When would you like to return?" Megan thought for a moment.

"Monday," she said. She would be fine, and she would be back in time to hear of her students' weekend, she thought. The clerk gave her some more recommendations for her stay before she left the counter.

She made it through security, grabbed a sandwich out of a machine for dinner and arrived at the flight's terminal with a few minutes to spare. She handed her small bag off to the flight attendant and boarded. It was a small plane with one seat on one side of the aisle and two seats on the other. She put her backpack under her seat and buckled her seatbelt. Just before the door was closed, a handsome gentleman in a suit, carrying a trench coat climbed on board and took his seat. Megan just barely noticed him. He sat a row behind her on the other side of the aisle. She nestled into her seat and leaned her head against the blue fabric. Flying used to make her nervous. That was when she had something to lose.

She looked out the window and watched the ground move slowly past her. This is one of the most impulsive and potentially stupid things she had done as Megan Rice. She was going toward the place from which she was forbidden. She decided she should get off the plane and go home to her one bedroom apartment where it was safe. She shifted in her seat. It was too late now - the plane was taxiing down the runway. She closed her eyes, put her head back on the seat and imagined how her life could be. She pulled a tie clip out of her pocket and rubbed the smooth gold with her thumb. She had taken it from Will's apartment the day she left to meet Mrs. Rawlings' lawyer. It's the only thing from her old life she had. An agent had returned it to her while she was in the safe house - probably because he felt sorry for her.

Two years had passed since she was Kristine. She wondered if she would be married to Will. She wondered what would have happened in her career. She never even saw her story in print. Did it win anything? She couldn't help but laugh a little to herself. How ironic. The story cost her everything, and she didn't even see it. Ralston Rawlings ended up going to prison for his part in the shootout, but his father somehow managed to escape prison time. All in all, it wasn't that surprising that Robert Rawlings walked around a free man

- his investors and board of directors ranged from high-powered business people to congress people to judicial members, none of whom wanted to be tied to a criminal. Megan shook her head in disbelief. He was the criminal, but she was the prisoner.

The plane bounced as it landed and roused Megan from her daydreams. It was almost nine o'clock Eastern Time. She set her watch forward as the plane taxied to the terminal. The airport was beyond small. It resembled an outhouse more than an airport. She avoided eye contact with the few other passengers and walked down the plane's stairs to the tarmac. She waited for her bag to be unloaded and then headed for the small building to get some information on a shuttle to the hotel the ticket agent recommended. She waited outside alone in the cold air for the van. She took a seat in the first row and looked out the window as others came out of the warmth of the building, climbed on and took their seats.

The shuttle wound up the mountain in the dark. There were three other people on the shuttle with her, but she didn't acknowledge them. She knew from the voices there were a young couple, probably newlyweds, and a man, probably there on business. She sat behind the driver and watched the lines on the road pass. Sleep began to creep up on her. Although she had only crossed one time zone, the day had been long and exhausting.

The van reached the little town on the mountain shortly after 10 o'clock. It stopped to drop off the couple at one of the first hotels. She waited in the van. Her hotel was the second stop, and since the man in the back of the van got off with her, she assumed it was the last stop. She hiked her bag onto her shoulder and found the reception desk.

"I don't have a reservation," she said.

"Oh, okay. Lucky for you we had a couple of

cancellations," the woman behind the counter said. "Smoking or non?"

"Non," Megan replied looking in her purse for a credit card.

"Okay," the woman said. Megan didn't even bother to look for the woman's name tag. "How many nights?"

"Three," Megan said.

"Okay. How would you like to pay for this?"

Megan handed her a credit card. She signed the receipt and took the room card. She walked through the lobby. There was a fireplace with several couches and chairs around it. Beyond the lobby area were a ski shop, which was closed, and a bar and a restaurant. Everything seemed rustic - made of wood. She found the elevators and rode up to her floor. She turned on the light, put her bags on the desk and looked around the room. It was quiet. She sighed. All those miles to escape loneliness and boredom and here she was - same problem, different state. She brushed her teeth, washed her face, slid out of her clothes and into bed.

* * * * *

The sun peeked through an open slot in the curtains. Megan rolled over to see the clock, which read 8:42. She thought about going back to sleep, but decided to see what the town had to offer. After all, that was the reason she left the comfort of her apartment. She showered, put on a pair of jeans, a long-sleeved white T-shirt, a royal blue sweatshirt and her water-proof snow shoes. She dried her now blonde hair and put on a little makeup. Although she would have preferred a weekend on a beach, she was used to cold weather. She looked at herself in the mirror. She didn't think she was as attractive as she used to be - maybe because her green eyes didn't gleam with life anymore. They actually resembled the lifeless eyes of the young bartender who helped save her life. No... She wouldn't let herself think about that - not this weekend.

She put her room card, Will's tie clip, some money, a credit card and her ID in her jeans pocket and perched a pair of sunglasses on her head. She left her room and made her way to the bar/restaurant she had seen last night. She found a table for two by the window over-looking the frozen lake. There were some skaters on the ice. Being President's Day weekend, the hotel and town weren't as crowded as they may be during a holiday when more people were off of work. A waiter approached her with a menu and a coffee pot.

"Good morning," he said.

"Hi," she said taking the menu.

"Coffee?"

"Yes, please," she said, and he turned the cup on the table over and filled it. Everything was white - the crisp linen tablecloth, the cup, the saucer and the backdrop out the window.

"I'll give you a couple of minutes to look over the menu," he said.

"That's okay - I don't need it. I'll just have some wheat toast and a scrambled egg," she said handing him the menu.

"Sure thing. Can I bring you a newspaper while you wait?" he asked. She thought for a second. Was she close enough to get the Chronicle? It was a nationally renowned paper. Will would be in his office at this time of the morning going over yesterday's issue.

"Um, okay," she said. She waited for the waiter to walk away and glanced around the restaurant. There weren't many people, but most were in couples or families. There was a lone man across the room. It was the man from the plane last night.

His salt and pepper hair was the only thing she could see as he read a paper and drank coffee. He seemed refined in his manners and his dress - like he came from money. He reminded her of Will - not so much in looks, but in the classy way he moved. He must have been the man in the van with her last night. She had a desire to introduce herself to the stranger but decided against it. Kristine may have marched right up to him and offered to buy him breakfast if she had the urge. Megan tried to melt into her surroundings.

She turned her head and watched the people on the ice. A man was helping a toddler learn how to skate. She smiled as she watched them. The waiter returned with her newspaper. It wasn't the Chronicle. Her heart flip-flopped in relief and disappointment. She read the paper with the eye of an English teacher and the heart of a reporter. She critiqued the stories and thought about what Kristine would have done differently. Her toast and eggs arrived before she could make her way through the second page. She folded the paper so she could continue reading while she ate.

There were stories about people dying, and she wondered if they were really dead. There were stories about tragedies all over the country and the world, and she wondered how much had been brought on the people by their own actions. Kristine was more of an optimist, but Megan was a cynic. She pushed the paper aside in disgust - mostly of herself. She finished her breakfast, signed the slip to charge it to her room and wiped the corners of her mouth with her napkin. She put the napkin on the table, breathed a sigh of resignation and stood up to leave. As she began across the dining room, she thought she caught the man with the salt and pepper hair watching her. It made her self-conscious and scared, so she walked a little faster. She tried to look straight ahead. When she finally made it to the lobby of the hotel, she decided to take a stroll through the little town.

The sun was warm, and the air was cold. They seemed to balance each other eliminating the need for a coat. She saw her reflection in windows, and she still didn't recognize herself at times. The blonde hair still made her do a double take. Megan browsed through some shops, but any time she considered making a purchase, she thought about how she may have to leave it behind some day. She would put whatever it was back on a shelf or a rack and leave quietly. She found a small book store, and bought a magazine and a book - a romance no less. Megan really was a different person from Kristine. Kristine Larkin would have rolled her eyes at someone who lost themselves in a romance novel. The magazine she purchased was news oriented, so she reasoned that Megan was just more balanced than Kristine. Maybe she was or maybe that's what she told herself to feel better.

She had walked to both ends of the town, which wasn't all that large. There was a coffee shop about two doors down from her hotel, so she back-tracked and bought a hot chocolate with extra whipped cream. She returned to the hotel lobby and forced herself to sit in front of the fire. Her initial thought was to go to her room and lie in the bed to read. She spent her days and nights at home doing just that or else she would get on her treadmill and run until she couldn't run any more. When she first bought the treadmill, she could only manage five or ten minutes before her lungs and legs gave up on her. After two years, she sometimes lost track of time and ran for hours. She was pretty sure that she could run one of those marathons now. Of course, Kristine thought anyone who wanted to run 26 miles was on the verge of insanity or was a masochist. Kristine avoided pain. Megan almost enjoyed pain, because she was numb most of the time. Feeling anything reminded her she was still technically alive.

The sofa was brown and overstuffed. She put her cup on the wood coffee table in front of the sofa and sank into the couch. Feeling self-conscious about her romance novel, she pulled the news magazine from the bag and began to read it. There were stories and editorials that stirred her insides. She wanted to find a computer and write. Sometimes she would sit for hours writing in her apartment. She deleted most of what she wrote just in case anyone ever broke into her apartment. She didn't want to reveal anything about herself. She even deleted the history on her web searches so no one could view them. She had always wanted to know what became of her story, but she never could work up the courage to find out. She tried to keep the memories of the story and the day she died buried deep. She would only let herself think about good memories or what possibilities Kristine's personal life had held.

The traffic in the lobby began to pick up as the afternoon turned to early evening. Megan finished her hot chocolate, which was now cold, then the magazine. Her stomach reminded her she hadn't eaten lunch, so Megan went upstairs to change for dinner. She put the magazine and book on the desk in her room. The couple on the book looked so beautiful and passionate as she ran her hand over the cover hoping some of their happiness would transfer to her even if only for a second. She was suddenly inspired to try to look pretty for no one other than herself.

Megan showered again. This time she spent some time on her hair rather than just blowing it dry with her fingers. She used a brush to add some body to it and then pulled the sides up into a clip. Makeup was something with which she hadn't taken much time since her days in New York. Derrick and Kristine would sometimes go to upscale makeup stores to try all the latest colors and products. Megan bought her makeup from one of those huge stores where you could get your tires rotated and buy laundry detergent. She managed as well as she could with the minimal products she had in her tiny cosmetics bag. Her green eyes were painted with a light brown eye shadow, lined and smudged with black eyeliner, and her long lashes were brushed with black mascara. She added some color to her cheeks and a hint of a nude color on her lips. She stepped back from the mirror and examined the person looking back at her. Although she admitted to herself this was the best she had looked in years, she still felt a little silly.

She had packed the only dress she owned. It was the stereo-typical little black dress for all occasions - short sleeves, round neck, fitted at the waist, and it fell to just above her knee. She could wear it to a funeral or a wedding if she knew anyone well enough to attend either of those events. She didn't know if she was too over-dressed for February at a ski resort, but she didn't care. The most important thing to her was to feel good again. She put on her black heels with the pointy toes and sling backs and looked in the mirror. There was something missing, but she knew no amount of makeup or a little black dress was going to put the light back in her eyes. She sighed, put her room key, lipstick and a few other items in the small black purse she had brought and went downstairs.

She had felt the heat of eyes on her in the hall, the elevator and the lobby and considered returning to the safety of her room. Maybe the attention she was getting wasn't worth it. Being there by herself caused her to stick out of the crowd. She swallowed hard and cleared her throat as she approached the hostess stand. "Table for one," she told the hostess.

"Great," she said looking at the chart on her podium. She was young and pretty. Megan immediately disliked her. "It's going to be about 10 to 15 minutes. Is that okay?"

"Sure," Megan said.

"Great. Name?" she said in a bubbly voice.

"Rice," Megan said quietly.

"Great! You can wait in the bar area," she said. Megan guessed everything was "great" to the hostess.

"Great," she said in reply and half mockingly.

Megan walked toward the bar area on her left. It was dark in the restaurant and bar, and it took her eyes a moment to adjust before she could make her way in to find a seat. She heard several men's voices boom in laughter. She hoped they hadn't laughed at her. She found the bar stool nearest to the door, but she never sat with her back to the door anymore. She walked down the long side of the bar. There were three people sitting next to each other talking with the bartender and couples on either side of them. She walked past them, rounded the corner and sat facing the door on one of the four stools along the short side of the bar. Had she been in a bar since that day? She swallowed hard and looked at the glass bottles lined up on the wall. She turned her hand over and looked at the tiny white scars on the palm of her hand where the doctors had picked out broken glass. Just as she was about to leave, the bartender walked up to her.

"What can I get you?" His voice startled her. She looked at him as he put a white square napkin on the bar in front of her. He didn't look anything like the bartender behind the counter that day.

"Um, nothing. I'm just waiting for a table," she said.

"Okay, let me know if you change your mind," he said.

"Wait!" she said quickly as he started to walk away. "I'm sorry. I changed my mind." The bartender walked back to her. "I'll have a glass of Merlot," she said rolling the corner of the napkin.

"Sure thing," he said. He walked away again and returned with a glass of wine.

"Thank you," she said only briefly glancing at him.

"You're welcome. My name's AJ. Just let me know if you need anything else," he said, and she nodded. He walked away, and she took a sip of her wine. She heard a boom of laughter come from the group along the long side of the bar. She looked up and saw a man she recognized. He had dark hair with heavy touches of grey. This was the same man from breakfast this morning, but she hadn't really seen his face until now. He took her breath away. He was movie star attractive in a Cary Grant meets Gregory Peck kind of way, only he was broader through the shoulders and maybe a little more muscular than the tall slender men of 50s Hollywood or like Will. She couldn't look away fast enough, and he caught her staring. She quickly went back to rolling the napkin, but couldn't get his face out of her mind. It was distinguished, full of life and oddly familiar. She wanted to look again at the stranger to make sure her eyes weren't playing tricks on her. She tried to think of a reason to look. She cleared her throat, straightened on her barstool and sought the bartender, who was talking with the stranger and the couple seated with him.

"Um, excuse me," she said her voice cracking from nerves, which caused her to involuntarily make a painful expression. The young man behind the bar smiled a sly, guy smile at the stranger and moved toward her. She managed only a glance at the man, who was in turn looking at her. She felt her face burn with embarrassment.

"What can I do for you?" the bartender asked and leaned up against the bar, both arms outstretched to brace himself as if he was going to do a pushup on the bar to impress her. Now that he was standing in front of her, she thought quickly for a reason.

"May I see a menu, please?" she replied thinking how stupid it sounded and shook her head ever so slightly in disgust. She shrank on her bar stool.

"The soup is great here," the stranger said from down the bar. She looked at him embarrassed by her transparency. He had seen through her meager attempt at finding an excuse to talk to him. She wanted to cry.

"Thank you. I'll have to try it," she said and took the menu from AJ when he returned. She opened it and hid her face behind it. She took a deep breath and remembered her fast talking, man-manipulating days. The days when she felt confident in herself and could work a man into giving her the details for a story even if it painted him in an unpleasant light. Maybe she was a completely different woman now. Her mind raced, and she didn't realize the bartender had returned.

"The gentleman would like to buy you another drink and a cup of soup," AJ said. She wanted to say yes, but fear overcame her.

"You know, I think I changed my mind," she said closing the menu. "I think I'm just going to have dinner in my room." She opened her purse for money and noticed herself shaking. She pulled out a fifty dollar bill, put it on the bar and stood to leave. She kept her head down to avoid looking at the man who had just offered to buy her dinner or at least a cup of soup.

"Whoa, let me get you some change," AJ said.

"No, that's okay," she said as the shaking entered her voice. "Keep it." She didn't want to have to stay there and wait for change. She walked as quickly as her heels would let her. She was used to gym shoes or flats now. As a reporter in New York, she could run down a street chasing a byline in three inch heels. Just as she started pushing the elevator button with relentlessness, she heard a voice.

"Hey, hey, hey," the man's voice said. She pushed harder and faster. "Hey," the man's voice said again taking her hand, and she unconsciously made a fist to hide the scars and what she was holding. "You're going to push that button right through the wall." She was shaking harder now and tried to pull away from him.

"I'm sorry," she whispered keeping her eyes on the pointy toes of her shoes.

"Hey, I'm sorry," he said. "I didn't mean to offend or upset you." She looked up, and the stranger from the bar was standing in front of her. He wasn't as tall as Will, but he was still about half a head taller than she was even with her heels. She guessed him to be 6'1 or 6'2. He was darker than the fair haired Will, and he was just as impressive in the light as he was in the bar. His eyes were dark and warm with long dark lashes. She didn't know what to say and realized she was staring at him. He was wearing a black turtleneck with a dark grey sport jacket over it and black dress pants with a black belt that had a classy, small silver buckle. He could have been a model in a magazine.

"No," she mustered in a weak voice. "I'm sorry. It's just that I'm not good around people." She thought about how that sounded and decided to add something to it. "I mean... I just... I'm painfully shy." She looked down, and her hand was still in his. It felt good. When was the last time she touched someone? His hand was large and warm. It swallowed her small hand - just like Will's.

"Well, again. I'm sorry," he said. "I should have known how shy you were from the plane and van."

"Plane and van? Were you sitting behind me?" she asked trying to hide the fact she had noticed.

"Yes. I also noticed you in the dining room this morning and reading in the lobby this afternoon," he said. Her heart pounded so hard she was sure he could hear it.

"Oh," she said hoping she hadn't done anything embarrassing like adjust her bra strap while he was watching.

The elevator dinged, and the door opened. She looked at it and then back at their hands. When had she pulled the tie clip out of her purse? "I was just going to eat in my room," she said quietly. He let go of her hand.

"Okay," he said. She stepped in the elevator, and as the door was closing, he put his arm up to stop it. "Or," he said. "You could come have dinner with me. I could help you overcome your shyness."

"I don't know," she said hesitantly.

"Look," he said. "You look absolutely amazing, and it's a shame to let the dress go to waste." She wasn't convinced. "And you don't have to say anything. You can just sit there and make all the men in the room extremely jealous of me." She laughed out loud.

"That's the worst line of crap I've ever heard," she felt the air fill her lungs and lift her spirit. He smiled at her. She hadn't felt this way since the few days she had with Will. She returned the smile.

"Fine. Then you'll have to listen to reason. You have to eat something," he said. "Come on." He offered her his arm. She tried to slip the tie clip in her purse without him noticing. She tentatively stepped forward and put her arm through his. "That's better. My name is Jack Hamilton."

"Nice to meet you, Jack," she said, and they stepped out of the elevator together.

* * * * *

Jack's table wasn't ready when they returned to the restaurant. So they went to the bar. AJ appeared with a fresh glass of wine for her. "I'm glad you came back," he said.

"Thanks," she said shyly and sat down on the stool.

"This guy is such a good tipper I was beginning to think he

was interested in me!" The group laughed, and Megan allowed herself a small, nervous laugh.

"Sorry, AJ. I don't think you could pull off this dress," Jack said, which brought another round of laughter. "I'd introduce you, but you didn't tell me your name," Jack said and put a reassuring hand on the small of her back.

"Oh, sorry. It's Megan. Megan Rice," she said suddenly feeling secure with his hand on her back.

"Everyone, this is Megan," Jack said. He introduced her to the couples. "And you know AJ," he added. She nodded and said hello to everyone. "So, we were talking about a story I read in the paper this morning before you came into the bar. Some group was trying to rank the worst songs ever." This brought more laughter.

"I still think you had the best one, Jack," Madison, one of the young females said flirtatiously. Megan could tell her husband didn't care, which amused her. "I never understood that muskrat song."

"Jack?" a female voice said from behind them. They all turned. It was the hostess. "Your table is ready."

"Okay, thanks, Jillie. Can they set it for two instead?" Jack asked and started to stand.

"For you? No problem," she said and left the bar. Megan noted how people responded to him. Women wanted his attention, and the men seemed to want to be his best friend. She was amused by this, yet she felt a shiver run down her spine.

Jack led her out to the reception area and waited for the hostess to collect another menu. They followed her through a dimly lit room with music playing softly. Each table had a white linen table cloth and an enclosed candle burning in the center. The sound of silverware clanking and the low murmur of voices filled the air. It was hard for Megan to believe this was the same bright dining room where she had breakfast.

Jillie led them to a table by the large windowed wall near where Jack had been sitting that morning. There were lights shinning on the ice outside, but there were only a few adult skaters. Jack held out her chair for her and helped her scoot into the table. He then moved to take his seat.

"It's beautiful here," she said quietly as she placed her napkin in her lap.

"Yes. It is," he said smiling. "So, Megan Rice have you ever been here?" She looked at him suspiciously and took a moment to consider her answer.

"No," she said and picked up the menu hoping it would stop any more questions.

"A woman of few words," he said smiling and picked up his menu. "You can talk when you're ready." They sat for a few moments studying the menu. She decided she needed to find out more about this man, so she closed her menu and put it on the table.

"Why are you here alone?" she asked abruptly.

"Okay. You want to cut to the chase," he said with a grin and closed his menu, too. His eyes wrinkled when he smiled. His teeth were white and straight. She couldn't believe she was sitting across from him. "I'm working," he said. She looked confused. "I'm checking out this place for a convention my company is considering having here."

"Where do you work?" she asked feeling a little like Kristine chasing a story.

"The government," he replied. She looked even more confused, and he laughed. "I'm a pencil pusher for the IRS. We like to meet each year before tax season to go over new information. I'm here scoping out this place for the end of the year."

"Oh," she said.

"Hey, don't sound so disappointed. I promise I won't audit you," he said still grinning. "Of course, I'm used to it. No one likes the IRS."

"I'm not a big fan of the government in general," she said without considering her words. "Isn't it tax season now? Shouldn't you be pushing a pencil?"

"Try not to hold it against me," he said leaning forward. "I don't actually do the auditing and stuff."

"I'll try," she said. He had an ease about him that made her want to relax. Still, she couldn't chance too much and wasn't even sure she knew how to relax anymore. "If you work for the IRS, why were you on my plane?"

"The IRS has offices all over. I was there on business." He said. She noticed it didn't take him long to answer so it wasn't as if he had to come up with one. "So, do I get to ask some questions now?" he asked. She thought for a moment. It may set off more alarms if she said no.

"You can try, but I'm not promising answers."

"Fair enough," he said. "So, why is a beautiful woman like you here by yourself?" She swallowed and prayed for someone to come take their order.

"I don't know," she stumbled for a reason. "I guess I don't have many friends. Like I said, I'm shy."

"Well, I'll consider it my lucky day then."

"I wouldn't count on getting *too* lucky today." She slapped a hand over her mouth when she realized what she had said and how sarcastic it sounded. He laughed at her. "I'm sorry. I shouldn't have said that."

"Why not?" he asked still laughing. "It was funny." She let herself smile. A waitress walked up to the table.

"Hi. I'm Christine, and I'll be taking care of you tonight." Megan's heart sank at her words. She looked at the young lady's name tag to make sure she heard her correctly. It was spelled differently, but the impact was the same. "Can I get you something from the bar or an appetizer?" Megan didn't hear another word.

"Megan?" Jack reached across the table.

"What?" she replied moving her arm out of the path of his hand.

"Are you okay? You're as white as this table cloth."

"Fine. I'm fine," she said.

"Do you want a drink?" he repeated.

"What? No," she said. "You know, I'm not feeling very well all of the sudden." She put the napkin on the table and stood.

"Uh, wait," he said. "I'll walk you to your room."

"No," she said. "I'll be fine." She walked quickly from the dining room and didn't chance waiting for the elevator. She took the stairs and ran up the three flights in her heels. She opened the door to her room. Most of the lights were on. Megan always left lights on - even when she slept. Tears ran down her face, and she couldn't catch her breath. She threw her purse on the dresser and then rushed after it. She pulled out the tie clip and threw herself on the bed. She sobbed until there were no more tears. She had had a student named Christine once, but it hadn't had this impact. Maybe it was because she was out of her comfort zone.

Her nose was stuffy, and she could feel the puffiness in her face and eyes. She stared at the ceiling thinking about how crazy she must have seemed. There was a knock on the door.

"Who is it?" she called with a voice that sounded like she had been crying. She stood up and walked to the door.

"It's Jack."

"Jack, now's not a good time," she said standing by the door.

"Megan, I just want to make sure you're okay. I'm not

going to be able to sleep tonight if I don't know you're okay. Please open the door." She closed her eyes and thought about it for a minute. "Come on, you really don't want to see me after a sleepless night. I'm really quite frightening."

"Hold on a minute," she said and went to the bathroom mirror. She looked awful with red, puffy eyes. She had cried off most of her makeup and what was left had run down her cheeks. She dampened a wash cloth and rubbed her face. She quickly blew her nose into a rough, thin, hotel tissue and went back to the door. She put her head down and opened the door.

"Can I come in for a minute?" he asked and walked past her before she could say no. She kept her head down and followed him. She leaned against the wall of the small entry way across from the bathroom. If he had been a couple of minutes later, she would have been asleep. He took a step toward her and lifted her face with his finger. She sniffled and tried to avoid looking into his eyes. "Want to talk about it? Maybe I can help."

"I'm fine," she insisted.

"Honey, you're anything but fine." He put his hand behind her neck as he spoke. "Did you know you're beautiful?" She made a sarcastic, short grunt. "You really are." He pulled her closer so her head was resting on his chest. He wrapped his arms around her. She took a deep breath. This was the safest she had felt since Will had held her. Still, she couldn't totally relax. "You deserve smiles and happiness, not tears and hiding in a hotel room," he said. "Let me help you," he whispered.

"I really wish you could," she said and then wished she hadn't. As safe and warm as she felt, she broke free from his hug and walked back to the door. She forced a smile and said, "I'm really fine now. I just needed a good cry. It was probably hormones or something," she said hating herself for using the irrational, hormonal woman excuse. He followed her to the door and stopped her before she could open it.

"I hope you'll feel better in the morning. Would you like to meet me for breakfast?"

She thought about it for a moment. "That would be nice."

He lifted her face, this time cradling it in both hands. "I'm right down the hall if you need me." She nodded, and he moved a little closer to her. He looked down at her and smiled. "Do you think it would be okay if I gave you a little kiss goodnight?" She nodded without even thinking. He leaned closer to her and gently brushed her lips with his. Her heart was pounding so hard she felt it in her throat. He kissed her again with more intensity, and she felt her legs weaken. He moved one hand away from her face and put an arm around her waist to hold her closer...and maybe hold her up. She managed to find the strength to pull him even closer as she returned the kiss. Her whole body pulsed with excitement. He pulled his lips away, and they both opened their eyes. "Wow," he whispered.

"That was a little kiss?" she asked when she finally found her voice.

"I think I better go before we do something you might regret," he replied with a smile.

"I would regret it?" she replied.

"Well, there's no way I would," he said as the smile widened. He moved closer to her and whispered, "And yes. That was a little kiss." He gave her a peck on the forehead and left her standing in the doorway.

* * * * *

She woke up on top of the covers still in her black dress. She ran her fingers over her lips and smiled at the memory of the kiss. Images of Will flashed through her mind, and a small part of her felt guilty for kissing Jack. She had spent her life as Megan fantasizing about Will and wanting to be with him. She wondered if Jack would replace Will in her fantasies when she returned home without either of them. Will would always have part of her heart whether she was Megan or Kristine. She shook her head. She was pathetic. She barely knew either of these men, and she was thinking of how they'd fill her dreams for the rest of her life. She let her mind go back to the events of last night.

Megan cringed when she thought about her reaction to hearing her old name. If she was going to have any joy in life, she couldn't stay on this course. The goal for the day: live a little.

Megan did her best to minimize the puffiness in her face and eyes and got ready for the day. She remembered she had agreed to meet Jack for breakfast, so she went to the dining room hoping she hadn't missed him. Her stomach rumbled so loudly in the elevator, she felt the need to give a weak smile to the elderly couple in there with her. It had been 24 hours since she had eaten anything. Between the hunger pangs and the butterflies at seeing Jack, she wondered if she'd even be able to eat anything.

As soon as she walked into the room, she saw Jack rise from a table and wave her to him. She couldn't control the smile on her face or the pounding in her chest. He was wearing jeans and a tan v-neck sweater with a white shirt under it. His salt and pepper hair was combed to the side.

"Look, I'm really sorry about last night," she said. He motioned for her to have a seat.

"Sorry about what?" he asked sitting.

"You know. The episode in here where I left you to eat alone," she said putting the napkin on her lap. "I was a maniac," she said trying to sound playful.

"We all have our moments," he said putting her at ease. "Paper?" he asked offering her the newspaper.

"No, thank you," she said not wanting to chance another panic attack. A waiter approached them. "I'll have coffee, pancakes, 2 eggs scrambled, hash browns and... some turkey sausage, please," she said before he could ask. The waiter turned over the coffee mug in front of her and poured her a cup.

"Sure. Would you like anything?" he asked Jack.

"I'll have the same, please," Jack said. He turned his attention to Megan as the waiter walked away. "Turkey sausage?"

"It's better for you."

"Good thinking. Counteract the pancakes, eggs and hash browns," he teased with a grin.

"I haven't eaten anything since yesterday morning," she explained. "I hope you weren't waiting long. I didn't know what time to meet you."

"Not long at all. Are you feeling better?" She was sipping her coffee, but nodded. She put the cup back on the saucer.

"Much, thanks," she said smiling. "You must have thought I was crazy," she laughed.

"Not at all," he said in a soothing tone that made her feel thankful to him. "I was worried about you, though. I'm glad you let me in to see you last night. I'd like to think that little kiss helped put you on the mend."

"Maybe it did," she said with a smile that lit up her face. "So, what are your plans today?"

"Well, I was thinking I'd like to do something with you," he said with a charm in his voice that made her smile at him. Actually, she couldn't stop smiling.

"I'd like that," she said and felt her face flush.

They made small talk while they ate their breakfast and

finished a second cup of coffee. She noticed his table manners - the napkin in his lap, elbows off the table - and thought someone had gently lectured him as a boy. Slowly, she became more and more comfortable with Jack. She didn't know if it was his manner or her losing the ability to hide behind her new persona. Her face began to hurt from the smiling and laughter - two things she wasn't used to doing. She actually caught herself flirting, too. The dishes were cleared, and she sat back in her seat.

"So, Megan, what do you do?" he asked as he watched her analyzing him.

"Why?" she replied on automatic pilot and cringed at her defense mechanisms.

"I'm interested, that's why." She thought about the question. It seemed harmless enough and something someone would normally ask. She already knew he worked for the IRS.

"I teach high school English," she said. Of course, there was no picture of her in a yearbook to prove it. She always missed her scheduled photo time. One of her fellow teachers even kidded her once about being in the witness protection program. She laughed off the comment and made a note to herself to steer clear of that teacher.

"I'm impressed," he said. She wrinkled her eyebrows.

"There's nothing impressive about that," she said dryly. Now being a reporter for a top-notch newspaper - that would have been impressive. Writing stories that touched people's lives would have been impressive. Spending your afternoons reading essays written by 18 year olds who didn't comprehend the concepts of a complete sentence or verb conjugation wasn't impressive at all.

"I think it's amazing. You're shaping the future," he said.

"Yeah, that's what I do," she laughed sarcastically. "These kids couldn't care less about my class. All they care about is text messaging, iPods, clothes and sex. Some of them are lucky they can spell their own names correctly thanks to texting."

"If you reach just one, is it worth it?" She had never thought about it. Suddenly, she felt better about her new life. Jack was making Megan's life seem livable, and she liked it. She liked him.

"Yeah, I guess it is," she nodded. There are worse things she could do with her life, she thought. "I just didn't picture my life turning out like this. So, tell me about you." She quickly changed the subject.

"My life isn't exactly what I had expected either. I don't know that anyone's is," he said, but she thought he had no idea how different her life really was.

"What did you think you'd be doing now?"

"I was raised by my aunt and uncle. I was determined to help people, so I went to medical school. I guess you could say life threw me a curve ball, and that's how I ended up where I am."

"Medical school? Wow! Talk about impressive. How far did you get?"

"As far as my rotations."

"That far!? What made you quit when you were so close? Was it lack of patients, because I can't think of any woman who would get undressed in front of you and actually admit there was something wrong with her." They both laughed.

"Some family stuff got in the way," he said.

"So you were raised by your aunt and uncle?" She used her journalism skills to broach the subject without flat out asking what happened to his parents.

"Yes. It was my mom's idea. She didn't think she could give me the kind of life my aunt and uncle could. My aunt couldn't have children."

"Wow. That was so selfless of her. She must love you very much."

"She did," he said quietly looking down at the table. Megan didn't want to dig further. "What do you say we get out of here and go skating?"

"Ice skating?" she asked smiling.

"Of course, ice skating," he replied playfully.

"I don't know how," she admitted.

"What about skiing?"

"Nope," she said with an embarrassed smile and shook her head.

"So you don't skate and you don't ski. Why are you here?" he asked playfully.

"I just wanted to get away. I can do warm weather stuff like play tennis, baseball, swimming, basketball...and I'm really good at some indoor sports," she said in a flirtatious way that surprised even her. He looked surprised, too.

"Well, okay then," he said. "Come on. I'll teach you some outdoor, winter activities," he stood and quickly helped her out of her seat. A phrase her mom used to tell her ran through her mind - if it seems too good to be true, it is. Megan tried to erase the thought, but in her heart she knew she had to be careful. Still, she wasn't looking for a long-term relationship...she couldn't. So what was the harm in having a little fun for a day? She tried to stop over-thinking everything.

"I'll give it a try," she said and let him take her arm in his.

They rented skates and a locker for their shoes. After they changed into the skates, he took their snow shoes and put them in the locker. He met her on the bench. The sunlight hit the snow and ice.

"Okay. Are you ready?" he asked standing.

"We're about to find out," she replied and stood up. She wobbled and grabbed a hold of his arms. She started laughing.

"I take it this isn't a good sign."

"Come on," he grinned and led her to the ice. He stepped out. She followed him and slid into him.

"Sorry!" she giggled.

"It's okay," he tightened his grip on her arms. He slowly skated backwards pulling her with him. She struggled to stay steady on the skates.

"Don't let go of me," she giggled.

"I promise," he said. He led her around the ice while people sped past them. A young boy, maybe seven years old, chased another boy around the rink.

"Does he have to make it look that easy?" she asked happily. "Little brat." They both laughed.

"Want to try to skate to me?" he asked.

"NO!" she said in a panic. She grabbed onto him tighter, and they wobbled until they lost their balance and landed in a clump on the ice. She tried to apologize, but they were both laughing so hard neither could speak. The laughter finally slowed. He leaned over and kissed her. She felt the warmth flow through her despite the fact she was melting ice with her rear end. "Maybe we should stick to things that won't result in broken bones."

"Or wet butts," he said smiling.

"Cold, wet butts," she added. He helped her to her feet and off the ice. They changed into their shoes. "This is much better," she said standing. The sun had disappeared behind clouds, so she raised her sunglasses on her head.

"How about a walk?" he asked.

"That sounds great, but I think I'm going to have to change clothes before my butt freezes into a solid block of ice," she said twisting to look at the darkened patch of denim.

"Gives new meaning to frosted buns," he said jokingly. "Let's change and meet in the lobby by the fire."

She practically skipped to her room and put on a dry pair of jeans, white thermal long-sleeved shirt and a navy sweater that zipped at the neck. She freshened up her makeup and noticed her eyes looked much better than they had that morning. She ran her fingers through her hair and gave it a quick spray. She noticed heavy snow falling outside, so she left her coat in the room figuring a walk would be out of the question.

The lobby was full of people mingling while seeking shelter from the snow storm. Jack was sitting on the couch in front of the fire.

"Hey," he said when he saw her approaching him. "A pretty bad snow storm blew in."

"I saw that," she said. He made room on the sofa for her, and she sat next to him. "I guess going for a walk is out of the question." She was disappointed. They were forced to sit closely because of the crowd. Her insides squirmed.

"I guess so," he said. "Actually, I think most outdoor activities are out of the question for awhile." She thought about his use of "outdoor activities" and decided she was too afraid to ask about indoor activities.

"Hm," she said staring into the fire. She pulled the sleeves of her sweater past her hands. She was more self-conscious than cold. They had shared an amazing morning and part of the afternoon. So why was she freaking out so much? She decided it was because with the lack of anything else to do, going back to his room was a real possibility.

"Cold?" he asked as he put his arm around her and rubbed the wool on her arm with his hand before she could answer. Still, it felt nice to be touched and held. "Better?" he asked, and she nodded. "Hey, relax," he said softly. She hadn't realized she had stiffened when he put his arm around her. "I don't bite."

"Sorry," she whispered and tried to ease her tense muscles.

She fought back a tear. How crazy was she? He was as sexy as Will, but he was real. Maybe that was the problem. He was too real. She let herself put her head on his shoulder. He leaned his head on hers. "This is kind of nice," she whispered.

"Mm hmm," he agreed. She snuggled into him.

"I had fun skating," she said.

"I don't think you can call what you did skating," he gently laughed.

"Hey, be nice," she giggled. This stranger was making her feel a little too comfortable.

"I am nice," he said.

"Jack?" she said sitting up a little. "What are we doing?"

"Sitting by the fire," he said.

"Seriously."

"Seriously? I don't know," he said. She put her head back down on his chest, and they sat quietly for a few moments. "I do want to get to know more about you," he finally said. These words caused her to stiffen. "Want to tell me about it?" he asked softly.

"Tell you what?" she replied innocently without moving. The warm comfort started to burn her. Anxiety took the place of peacefulness.

"Why you're always so scared. You're hiding something. Something pretty serious," he said holding her tighter. She sat up, lifted her head and shifted slightly away from him.

"Why do you think I'm scared or hiding something?" she said sounding a bit too defensive. "I'm not. Why would I be hiding anything? My life is boring. It really is." This could be the definition of protesting too much, she thought. That thought only made things worse, and her hands began to fidget as her eyes darted around the room.

"I don't know you very well, but you are by far the jumpiest person I've ever met. It goes way beyond shyness to sheer terror sometimes," he said. She could feel the color flood her face. She swallowed hard. She didn't know if she was mad or hurt or embarrassed. Maybe she was all of them.

"So you've picked up a lot of women in hotels, and that makes you an expert on how I'm supposed to act?" she asked angrily. He tried to speak, but she didn't let him. "Look, I don't know anything about you. I came here for a nice, quiet weekend and didn't want to meet anyone, much less some snake who preys on single women. What was I supposed to do, jump you right on the bar the night we met? Sorry to disappoint you, but you are resistible." She stood up. He was looking at her speechless, and she thought maybe she saw the hint of a smile fighting to pull his lips toward his eyes. This only infuriated her more. She lowered her voice and said, "By the way, aren't you getting a little old to play the predator?" She turned and rushed to the stairwell.

She took the stairs two at a time until she flung the door to the third floor open. She went into her room and paced the small area between the bed, window and door. She knew she had completely flown off the handle and attacked Jack. Old habits died hard. She flung herself onto the bed, leaned against the headboard and pulled her knees up to her chest. She rocked a little as she cried. She should never have taken this trip, she thought to herself. She got up and pulled her bag out and started to pack. She stopped and picked up the phone. "I need a ride to the airport."

"I'm sorry ma'am. We're not running the shuttle due to the storm," a young woman said.

"Then can you get me a taxi? I really need to catch a flight," she said picking at a piece of string hanging from her sweater.

"Ma'am, I don't think you'll find a driver willing to make the drive in this storm, and if you do, you'd be lucky to get a flight. You'd be stuck at the airport," she said.

"Thanks anyway," Megan said and put the phone back on the cradle. She plopped on the edge of the bed. Being stuck at the airport was better than being stuck here, she thought. Still, it was clear she wasn't going to find anyone to take her. Her plane left tomorrow evening anyway. She would just stay in her room. She looked at the clock. It was only 5:00. She fell backward on the bed and stared at the ceiling. She felt numb. She closed her eyes.

When she woke, she sat up on her elbows and looked at the clock. Great. Only two hours had passed. She had kind of wished a couple of years had passed. She moaned and got out of the bed. She changed into a pair of sweats and gym shoes, put her iPod into her pocket and headed for the door as she pulled her hair into a pony tail. She listened. It was quiet. She peeked out. No one. She scurried to the stairwell and took it to the bottom floor of the lodge. She had noticed on the elevator buttons there was a fitness center in the basement.

The wall and doors to the fitness center were glass. She slowed and made sure Jack was no where in sight. There was a young lady, maybe in her early 20s on the elliptical machine reading a magazine and listening to an MP3 player. A man near her age was using the nautilus equipment. They were probably a couple, she thought. There was an older gentleman on the recumbent bike reading a book. Megan walked in and avoided eye contact. She picked up a clean towel from a stack against the wall. She put the ear buds into her ears, took the iPod off hold, pushed the button, and rolled the dial to crank the volume. She climbed onto one of the two treadmills and adjusted the speed. She started out at a fast walk. After a few minutes of walking, she increased the speed so she was jogging. A few more minutes passed, and she increased the speed so she was running. She focused her eyes at a spot on the mirror so she didn't have to look at herself or anyone else. She ran.

She used the towel to wipe her face periodically. Motion too close to her startled her. She glanced around in the mirror.

"Miss?" a young man in shorts and a t-shirt said. She hit the button on the treadmill and slowed to a walk. She pulled one of the ear buds from here ear.

"Yes?"

"I'm sorry, but the center closes at nine. I just wanted to let you know you have less than 15 minutes," he said. She looked at the clock on the wall and then at the timer on the treadmill. She had been running for over an hour and a half.

"Okay, thanks. I'm finishing up anyway," she walked for a few minutes and climbed off the treadmill. A couple of years ago, she used her gym shoes to get her from city street to city street. She never dreamed of exercising like this. She found a place to stretch. Unfortunately for her life and fortunately for her health, this wasn't the first time she'd let her mind go blank and lost track of time on a treadmill. She was mad at herself for doing it in a strange place, though. Usually, she was in the security of her living room.

She left the fitness center and took the stairs back to the third floor. Quietly and carefully, she peeked through the door and looked down the hall. There was a couple waiting for the elevator. Other than that, she had a clear path to her room. She walked to her room and let herself in. The lights were on, of course, and she took a quick survey to make sure no one was hiding in the closet. She shook her head in disgust of her paranoia. She stripped off her clothes and took a hot shower.

She dressed in her jeans and a sweatshirt and called for room service. After an hour and a half of running, she didn't feel the least bit guilty about ordering the cheeseburger and fries. Plus, she thought to herself, she had ordered a diet drink and three bottles of water. She smiled and mumbled, "Female logic." She dried her hair and pulled it back into a ponytail.

She spent time savoring the burger and fries while she mindlessly flipped through the TV stations. By 11, she was ready to go to bed.

* * * * *

A knock on the door woke her. She wasn't sure how long she had been asleep. Maybe it wasn't a knock. She shivered. Another knock. She realized the room was dark and reached for the lamp. She never slept in a dark room. Then she noticed the chill in the room. "Hold on," she called as she stumbled out of the bed. She flipped the light switch by the door on and off and on and off. Nothing. She didn't know if she should be afraid. "Who is it?"

"Jack." Came a familiar voice. She hesitated for a second. "Come on. Open up." She shivered again and spontaneously opened the door. Maybe she was too cold to be cautious. She squinted from a blast of light. It didn't come from the hall, but a single light source. "Sorry," Jack said and moved the flashlight away from her face.

"No. I'm the one who should apologize," she said leaning on the door. "I was out of control before. Why is it so cold?"

"The electricity's out because of the snow and the generator won't kick on for some reason. I brought you these," he said as he extended a couple of blankets and a flashlight. She took them and cleared her throat.

"Um, thank you, but don't you need these?" He shook his head. His hair was ruffled as though he too had been sleeping in the time that had passed since she flew into her rage. He had on what looked like a dark blue t-shirt and plaid flannel pants with a drawstring at the waist. He held his flashlight as she stood in the doorway with the supplies.

"No, I got extra for you. They're handing them out downstairs to anyone who wants them. I took a chance you hadn't noticed the cold yet." She was touched by the genuine tone in his voice.

"But, I was so mean to you," she said. "Why would you be nice to me?" He looked down at the floor for a minute. She could tell he was considering his answer.

"Well, obviously something terrible happened to you. Maybe I'm trying to restore your faith in mankind. Maybe it's my job to protect you," he said. "I'm really not a bad guy."

"I'm so sorry about before. I tend to get defensive sometimes," she said and smiled at him as if to wave a white flag. The cold cut through her. She hugged the blankets to her and added, "This is the nicest thing anyone's done for me in a very long time."

"Well, it shouldn't be," he said quietly and paused. "Uh, the manager said it should only be another half hour before they get the generator running. There's a fire and some people in the lobby keeping warm if you want to go down."

"Oh, if it's only going to take a little while longer, I may try to sleep through it," she said not wanting to get dressed and listen to a bunch of people who didn't know the meaning of having a difficult life whine about the conditions.

"Okay. If you need anything, give me a call. I'm right down the hall," he said as he pointed his flashlight in the direction of his room. "I'll let you get back to sleep." He turned to follow the flashlight.

"Um, Jack," she called in a shaky voice with a hint of desperation. She wasn't sure what was going to come out of her mouth next. He stopped and turned toward her.

"What if they don't get the generator going soon?" she asked.

"Uh, I don't know," he said with a look of confusion. This was her last night here, she thought. Her last shot at doing something spontaneous and wild, and her last chance to make a memory to last her a lifetime.

"It could get even colder, couldn't it?" she asked.

"I guess," he said taking a step back toward her.

"Would you like to come in…here…with me?" she offered nearly crying as she spoke. "We could keep each other warm," she said trying to put reason behind her words. She was too afraid and unsure of herself to sound seductive. Jack gave her a weak smile.

"But that would make me exactly what you accused me of being," he replied. "I think I better go back to my room." She felt a tear fall down her cheek and hoped he hadn't seen it. Now she was embarrassed beyond words but slightly relieved. "Goodnight," he said and turned away.

She closed the door, went back to bed and huddled under the covers. At first she felt embarrassed by her brazen question. Then she felt hurt he'd rejected her. Finally, she was mad. He was the one who had come after her in the bar. The lights flickered on and the heat began to pump through the room. She hadn't offered herself to a man in what seemed like two lifetimes. Forget him, she thought. He's not worth the effort. What had she been thinking? She hadn't been thinking…that was the problem. That was the last time that would happen, she thought to herself.

Her mind raced through the night, and she felt relief when the sun started to peek through the gap in the blackout curtains. She was going home today. Although she took comfort in the thought she would be returning to her familiar surroundings, she felt like she was returning to prison. She also felt like she squandered her weekend pass.

Chapter Eight

The new snow was beautiful, she decided as she gazed out her window. She had already showered and called the front desk to find out when the first shuttle left for the airport. She pulled herself away from the wintery scene, put her hair dryer in her bag and zipped it. Taking one last look around the room, she checked out using the remote control on her TV. She left the key on the desk, put her backpack on her shoulder, grabbed her other bag and left the room.

She took the stairs to avoid the people standing at the elevators. In the lobby, she asked the young man behind the desk to keep her bag and send someone into the dining room to get her when the shuttle arrived. She peeked into the restaurant to make sure Jack wasn't there before she went in to get some breakfast and find a table.

Once she found the most secluded table, she ordered a cup of coffee, a bagel and some fruit. She sat facing the door so she would see him before he saw her. Moments from the weekend played through her head over and over again.

Jack walked into the dining room about 10 minutes after Megan had finished her breakfast. He looked tired, and she was glad. The clerk from behind the front desk startled her. A shuttle was ready. She waited for Jack to sit down before she made her move for the door.

She stood up, put her backpack on her shoulder and kept her eyes on the door. She tried not to move too quickly as to draw attention to herself. Out of the corner of her eye, she saw Jack stand. She moved faster. He called her name, but she kept walking.

There was a person standing at the front desk blocking her from getting her bag. She swayed eagerly, but Jack caught up to her while she waited.

"Megan, please wait. I need to talk to you," he said taking her arm. She pulled away and ignored him. "Please, Megan."

She managed to quietly say, "Don't do this to me. Just let me go."

"I can't," he said. The man in front of her finished his business and moved away.

"Hi. Can I get my bag please?" she said to the clerk. The clerk handed her the duffle bag, and she started for the van. Jack quickly got his bag from the clerk and ran out after her.

The van driver loaded her stuff in the back of the maroon van as she went around the side, got in and slammed the door behind her hoping it would lock automatically. It didn't. Jack opened the door and climbed into the bench seat behind her. Now she felt trapped. The van driver got into the driver's seat and started the engine.

"Wait! I want to get out," she said sliding across the seat. Jack and Megan were the only two passengers on the van.

"Then I do, too," Jack said. Defeated, she slammed herself back into the seat and turned her head to look out the window.

"Are we coming or going?" the driver asked looking in the rearview mirror.

"Coming with you," she grumbled. She dug through her backpack for her iPod and put on the earphones to try to drown out his voice.

"What about you?" the driver asked Jack.

"Yeah, go ahead," he said, and the man put the van into gear and pulled out from the curb. Jack touched Megan's shoulder, but she jerked away from him. "Look, I'm sorry," he said. "I never meant to hurt you."

"Can't hear you," she said but then pulled out the ear buds. "Hurt me?" she snorted. "I think you over estimate yourself."

"Look, you don't know the whole story," Jack said and

looked toward the driver. "I need to talk to you in a more….a more private setting."

"No second chances," she said folding her arms in front of her chest.

"Just let me talk and you listen. When you hear what I have to tell you, you'll understand everything." She looked out the window and noticed they were going a little fast for the sharp downhill curves and fresh snow fall.

"Are you married?" she asked softly and distantly.

"No," he said.

"Life threatening illness?"

"No."

"Sexually transmitted disease?"

"No," he laughed.

"Gay?"

"No."

"Not attracted to me?"

"Oh hell no!"

"Well, what is it then?" she asked irritated. Suddenly, they were both thrown up against the glass window as the driver took a sharp corner at a high rate of speed.

"Hey, put your seatbelt on," Jack said. Megan immediately wanted to do the opposite of what Jack told her, but the van seemed to be going a little fast so she did it anyway. The driver took another curve too quickly, and Jack slid across the van seat. "Do you want to slow down a little bit up there?"

"Just doing my job, Jack," the driver said. She heard Jack mutter the words "son of a bitch" as he flashed past her eyes and flew over her seat toward the driver. Megan sat up in her seat. Jack was fighting with the driver for control of the van as they swerved back and forth on the roadway.

"What the hell are you doing?" she screamed at the men as they struggled for control of the van. She tried to grab at Jack to pull him back. "You're going to get us all killed!"

Jack punched the driver so hard blood spattered on the window. The van picked up speed as Jack tried to pull the driver away from the wheel. Megan screamed, "Stop it!" She couldn't see the road because they blocked her view out the windshield. She heard a crash, and the next thing she felt was weightlessness. The two men were still fighting as the van flew off the side of the road. The only thing she could think to do was get into the crash position as they instruct you to do on planes, so she put her head between her knees and covered her head with her hands. She closed her eyes.

* * * * *

When she opened her eyes, she wasn't sure where she was or how she got there. She was on her side with her head in snow. She looked around and moved slowly. She remembered flying through the air. She tasted blood. Everything was quiet. She lifted her hand, which had blood on it.

"Jack?" she said in a whisper, still trying to find her voice. She cleared her throat and tried again. "Jack," she said louder this time. What if he was dead? She panicked. She unhooked her seat belt and tried to figure out which way she should go to get out of the van. She made her way toward where the windshield had been and saw the driver pinned against the steering wheel. She climbed to him and shook his arm. "Mister?" She pulled him away from the steering wheel, and the cold dead eyes from the bar flashed in front of her. She started shaking. She had an eerie feeling that everything was starting again. She scrambled to get away from it. She climbed out of the van, slicing her hand on broken glass in the windshield and scratching her face on a tree limb that was hanging from it. She fell out into the snow and started to crawl gagging for air. The cold snow and a drop of blood from her face brought her back to her senses. She turned onto her rear and took in the incredible mess that was once the van. She was surprised she made it out alive. What about Jack? She struggled to stand in the snow and slowly walked back to the van. She saw the dead man and shivered. She searched the wreckage next to him and didn't see any sign of Jack. She glanced back where she had been sitting and nothing. What if he was pinned under the van? She heard something and quickly looked around. There it was again. It was her name, and it was Jack. She raised her eyes to the trail the van had followed when it fell from the air and rolled down an embankment.

"Jack," she called and saw him stumbling through the snow toward her. She made it around the van and started to climb toward him. He slid the rest of the way to her. He took her head in his hands and immediately started asking her what hurt and looked at her cuts and scrapes. He, too, was bleeding from a cut on his face and had what looked like pine tree pieces in his hair.

"Thank God," he said and hugged her hard.

"Were you trying to kill us?" she yelled pulling away and slapping his jacket. "Ouch," she yelped as she noticed the gash in her hand from the windshield. He grabbed it and studied it. He used some snow to wipe her hand and face so he could get a better look at her most serious wounds.

"Your hand is really bad," he said and started walking toward the van.

"Yeah, well the driver's dead," she said sarcastically calling after him. He seemed only moderately affected by the news. "Don't you care?" she asked as he found their bags and started digging through them for something to wrap around her hand. "This guy had a mom, a dad, maybe a wife and kids," she said trying to provoke a response. This got his attention.

"You're right," he looked up toward the trail the van took and the road it left behind. "We're going to have to move," he dumped out their bags into the snow, and she protested. He found a white t-shirt in his bag and brought it over to her. He wrapped her hand with the shirt, and said, "Try to keep some pressure on it." He went back to rummaging through their belongings.

"What are you doing?" she asked impatiently. He ignored her and went on looking for supplies. "Will you at least tell me what you're doing so I can help you?" He paused and looked at her.

"See if you can find a first aid kit or a flashlight. Oh, and maybe matches or a map or something," he said. She stood there looking at him. "Go," he said and pointed to the van. She didn't know why she did it, but she did. She found a flashlight in the glove compartment and the first aid kit under the passenger's seat. She found a lighter in a pack of cigarettes in the visor above the dead driver. The only thing she didn't find was the map. Jack was stuffing items into their backpacks when she returned. He took the items from her and put everything but the lighter into one of the bags. He took the lighter and put it in his jean pocket. "Good," he said and zipped them. "Come on," he said and took her uninjured hand. He started leading her toward the woods, and she slightly tugged at him.

"Wait. Where are you going? The road's that way," she said, but he ignored her. "We can't just leave him here," she added pulling him harder. He stopped and turned around.

"You're going to have to trust me on this. I think we'll find help faster this way rather than trying to track up the side of that hill. It's too steep, and it could be days before anyone finds us down here," he said.

"But the lodge will notice when the van doesn't return and send help," she protested.

"They have more than one shuttle service running. They'll just think this guy took the day off. There are more resorts and private cabins this way. If we wait here in the open, we could freeze or you could bleed to death. Please, Megan. You have to trust me on this," he said almost pleading with her. It still didn't make sense to her, but it seemed important enough to him. Her head and hand hurt.

"Okay," she said thinking she'd be able to re-trace her footsteps if she needed to later. Maybe he knew what he was doing. He led her about 50 yards into the forest before he told her to sit down. The trees had blocked some of the snow from falling to the ground so it wasn't as deep inside the shelter. He grabbed the first aid kit and rummaged through it taking out some gauze and tape. He removed the shirt, which was soaked with blood on one side. He wrapped her hand with the gauze and secured it with the tape. He pulled a glove out of one of the bags and put it on her hand. "The glove will be tight with the bandaging. It might help stop the bleeding. Try to keep it elevated." She just watched him. Then he took another piece of gauze and put it to her forehead. He secured it with tape also. He was concentrating so hard she could see the veins in his forehead. He stood up, put the opened wrappings from the gauze back into the kit and closed it.

"Rest here for a minute. I'll be back," he said and turned. She sat and waited. He was gone for what seemed like a long time. She began to recall the moments before the van plummeted off the side of the mountain. Had she heard the driver call Jack by name? Is that what sent Jack lunging after him? If so, who was Jack? He said he worked for the IRS. How did a man who made it all the way to internships in medical school end up working for the Internal Revenue

Service? She sniffed the air. It smelled like smoke. She looked around and started walking back toward the accident. As she neared the edge of the forest, she saw Jack using a large branch to roughen up the snow all around the perimeter of the van so no footprints were visible. The van was on fire. She turned around and went back to where he had left her.

Her mind raced. What was going on? Who was this guy? Why was he burning the van? Why was she so drawn to him and willing to follow him into the forest when she knew their best hope was to go up the hill or wait until someone saw the smoke from the van. She glanced in the direction of the van and then grabbed Jack's backpack. She unzipped it and began going through it looking for clues as to who Jack Hamilton really was.

"What are you looking for?" a voice asked from behind her. She involuntarily jumped at the unexpected interruption.

"I, uh, I was looking for lip balm," she replied thinking quickly. "My lips are getting chapped in the cold air."

"And you thought I looked like the lip balm kind of guy?" he said taking the bag from her. He didn't sound upset, she noted. He sounded like he was amused and maybe even flirting.

"You never know," she said. "Can't always judge a book by its cover."

"True. We should go," he said and put the backpack on his back.

"Yeah, in a second. Why did you go back to the van?" she asked.

"I forgot to check for a cell phone or a radio," he said. She didn't own a cell phone anymore - no one to call and no one to call her.

"Don't you have one?" she replied.

"Lost it when I was rolling down the hill, I guess," he

answered.

"Where are we going again?" she said without standing.

"We're looking for another lodge, a cabin or the road," he said. "Come on."

"Don't you think we'd have a better chance getting rescued by the people who will show up to put out the fire you started?" she asked. He grinned. He seemed impressed by her.

"I'm not sure we want to be found by those people," he said.

"What kind of people are those?" she asked.

"That's something I needed to tell you," he said.

"Start talking, because I'm not going anywhere with you until I get some answers," she said planted firmly on the ground. "Why did the driver know your name?"

"You caught that, did you? Nice work."

"That's not an answer," she said and raised an eyebrow and crossed her arms in front of her.

"My name's on my luggage," he said. "And there's something else. Remember when I told you I worked for the government?" he asked. She nodded. "Well, I'm not exactly part of the IRS."

"What does 'not exactly' mean?"

"Can we walk and talk at the same time?" he asked reaching out a hand to help her off the ground. She looked at it and thought about it for a second. Her head was telling her to run out into the area where the van was burning and yell for help. Her heart was telling her to take his hand and follow him. Wait...that might have been her hormones. So what was her gut telling her? It told her to go with him. It told her those big brown eyes weren't lying now.

"Okay," she said and took his hand. She put her backpack on her back, and they began through the trees and climbing over broken limbs. "I'm listening." He walked first, holding branches so they wouldn't hit her face and taking her arm as they worked their way over the tree limbs and down slopes.

"I'm actually more of a government law enforcement official," he said.

"You're FBI?"

"If you want to get specific, yes," he answered.

"Great," she said disappointed and disgusted. "What else?"

"Well, that guy in the van may have been someone from a case," he said.

"So he's after you?" she asked cautiously while considering the other option.

"Maybe," he said.

"Well, if he's not after you," she said stopping. "Who is he after?" He stopped and looked into her green eyes. The fear and vulnerability bubbled to the surface as she looked at him.

"Look," he said breathing a little heavily from the day's stresses. "He may have been after me or... Or, he could have just been driving drunk."

"You drove us off a cliff because he was 'probably' after you or he had a few too many?" He wasn't telling her something. "I don't believe you."

"Come on. We have to keep moving," he said.

"I'm not going anywhere else with you until you tell me what's going on," she said. He looked down at her hand.

"You've bled through the bandaging and glove," he said taking her hand. "We have to get you somewhere so I can fix this," he said holding her hand in his. "Please trust me. I wouldn't do anything to hurt you. I know what I'm doing." She studied him as he spoke.

"Okay," she said. "But as soon as we get somewhere safe, you have to tell me what's going on." He nodded.

"Try to keep pressure on this and keep it elevated," he said and turned to continue.

He was methodical in his movements as he picked through the heavily wooded forest. Finally, after what seemed like hours of walking, climbing over and ducking under tree limbs, he stopped and looked around.

"Let's take a break for a couple of minutes," he said as he looked at his watch. She slumped against a tree and slid down it.

"Do you have any idea where we are or where we're going?" she asked.

"We've walked miles. There has to be something else on this God-forsaken mountain besides that town," he said sounding more agitated than he had.

"Let me get this straight. We're on the side of a mountain, hurt because you drove us off the road, we're lost, we're cold and hungry, and you don't have a clue as to what to do next?"

"We have to keep moving," he said. She knew he was right. Moving would at least keep them from freezing to death - for awhile anyway. She began to question whether he really knew what he was doing.

* * * * *

Just as she began to worry they were going to have to spend the night walking, they came to a small clearing. Jack put out his arm to stop her from going any farther. In the middle of the clearing was a small log cabin.

"Stay here," Jack whispered. The snow was deeper in the clearing. He made his way to the cabin and looked through the spaces in the boarded up windows. He walked back to her. "Okay. It's empty. We can stay here tonight."

They walked to the cabin and when Jack made it to the front door he saw a pad lock on it. He picked up a couple of sticks to try to break the lock, but they weren't strong enough.

He found a rock and began banging the lock. Megan rolled her eyes and walked around the cabin. All the windows were boarded, except for one in the back. It was just above a stack of firewood. The owner probably couldn't reach the window because of the wood. She climbed up the wood and tried the window. It wasn't locked. The window was small, but she made it in. She closed the window behind her, unlocked the deadbolt on the back door and wondered what kind of moron took so much time to close up a cabin and doesn't lock a window. Jack kept banging on the lock. She took off her backpack and put it on the kitchen table, which was covered with a sheet. The cabin had non-perishable items in the kitchen cabinets and was stocked with some men's clothes and blankets in the bedroom closet. There was a small bedroom and a bathroom. She tried the faucet, but there was no water.

Megan walked out the back door and around to the front where Jack continued working on the lock.

"Want help?" she asked over his shoulder. He turned around.

"You think you can get us in here?" he replied. She shrugged. "Then, be my guest."

"I can't get that lock off of there," she said matter-of-factly.

"Thank you," he grunted.

"And neither will you without bringing down this mountain of snow, Einstein," she said confidently.

"Do you have a point or are you just torturing me?" he said frustrated.

"I would have opened the door for you, but it's locked from the outside," she said. "The place is small but nice. Want me to show you around?" She turned in one triumphant move and crunched back through the snow. He threw the rock down and followed her. She opened the back door and walked into the cabin. Jack followed her and put his backpack on the table next to hers. "Impressed, FBI guy?"

"Embarrassed is more like it," he replied. He checked the wood burning stove in the center of the room. "I'll start a fire, and it should warm this place up quickly. I don't think we'll have to worry about the smoke, besides if we don't make a fire we could freeze in here. The night sky is going to be pretty black with the cloud cover."

"There's food in the kitchen and blankets in the bedroom," she said. She went to the kitchen to look for food.

"How long have you been in here?"

"Long enough to get a headache from all that banging you were doing," she said. "'Trust me,' he said. I must be an idiot to follow around a strange man just because he says, 'trust me.'"

"Okay, maybe I deserve that," he said and began to look around for himself.

"You probably do. You drive us off a cliff, won't tell me what's going on and if it hadn't been for this cabin, may have gotten us frozen," she said.

"I'm getting the impression this is going to be our first real fight," he said sarcastically. "What's your problem?"

"Nothing," she said slamming a cabinet closed, and then thoughts spilled out of her like an exploding box of spaghetti. "You are infuriating. You come on to me, make all nice and then throw up a brick wall. I ask you questions, and you either lie or avoid them with the 'trust me' crap. From now on, you earn trust. It's not free."

"Are you finished?" he asked impatiently.

"No," she replied confidently. Her head started spinning, and she swayed. He reached for her, but she pulled away and steadied herself using the kitchen counter.

"Let me help you to the sofa," he said reaching for her again. "You need stitches and something to eat," he said as she let him help her to the sofa. "With as much blood as you've lost, I'm surprised you're still standing at all." She grunted in return. Once she was safely on the sofa, he went back to the kitchen and began opening cabinets. He found some bottles of alcohol - vodka, brandy, whiskey. He took them out and put them on the counter.

"Make me one while you're at it. I could use a drink," she said only half jokingly.

He walked past her and into the bedroom. She was curious now but didn't want him to know. She heard some ripping noises. He appeared with some white cloth and went to get the bottle of whiskey. He twisted off the cap and handed her the bottle.

"No glass," she asked. "Kind of primitive, but it all ends up in the same place." She took a drink. She didn't like hard liquor, and the burn made her eyes water. He took the bottle back from her and dumped some onto the cloth. "What are you doing?" she asked, and he handed the bottle back to her.

"Keep drinking it," he said and pushed her hair away from the cut on her forehead so he could remove the gauze. He gently blotted at the dried blood and the cut. She flinched and yelped.

"That hurts like hell!" she cried.

"That's what the whiskey is for - pain and antiseptic." He began to remove the bandaging around her hand, but she instinctively pulled away like a toddler about to get a dose of medicine. "I need to see how deep this cut is," he said. "I don't think your forehead needs stitches." She sat quietly and watched him. He liked this doctor stuff she could tell. He was all business. She took more swigs of the liquor, and it eventually started to take the edge off the pain. She was growing more and more tired. He stood up, and she closed her eyes.

She opened them again when she heard him return. He brought her some blankets from the bedroom. "I found a needle and fishing line. I'm going to use them to close up your hand. First, would you consider getting out of those wet clothes?" he asked as he handed the blankets to her.

He was right, they were wet and cold. She replied with a gruff, "Maybe," and stood up. The alcohol rushed to her head, and she swayed again. He reached for her, and she pulled away, "I can do it myself," she said independently and defiantly. Staggering to the bedroom, she found some men's flannel shirts and a couple pair of jeans. There were a couple of sweaters and sweatshirts. She put on a flannel shirt and a sweatshirt over it. She pulled on a pair of jeans as best she could with her injured hand and looked for socks. She found a drawer with about five pairs rolled into balls. She pulled out two and put them on. She looked ridiculous. The clothes were several sizes too large, but she was warmer. She walked out of the room with Will's tie clip in her right hand and said, "There's some more for you." She plopped back down on the couch and wrapped up in the blankets. She took a few more swigs and didn't even notice the burn. Jack had built a fire while she changed. It hadn't quite caught yet, but the little warmth it provided was very welcomed.

He came out of the bedroom a few minutes later looking very rugged and handsome. He picked up the fishing line from the coffee table and sat on the edge of the couch.

"Keep drinking," he said. "This is probably going to hurt like hell."

"That's not exactly what I want to hear," she said slurring a word or two. "Can't we just wait? It's not that bad," she lied. She knew it was bad.

"No. We can't wait. I don't want you to lose any more blood," he said. "I don't know how long it's going to take us to find help."

"Fine," she said reluctantly. "Do you know what you're doing?"

"Yes, but I wish I had better light and a more sterile environment," he said looking around. "Let's go to the kitchen sink so I can pour this over it." He helped her stand and walked her to the sink. She was beginning to feel the effects of the day's events mix with the alcohol. She rubbed the tie clip with the thumb of her right hand. She wanted to pass out. "I'll get you a chair to sit on so you...uh, will be more comfortable," he said.

She sat in the chair, and he positioned her arm on the counter so her hand was over the sink. "Did you get hurt," she asked quietly.

"I might have some broken ribs... maybe a concussion and some scratches. I'm fine," he said. Threading the needle wasn't an easy task for his big fingers. Once he was finished with that, he began asking questions. "Where would you go if you could go anywhere in the world?"

She had seen this before on many of her reporting assignments in an emergency room. Take the patient's mind off what is happening. Maybe he did know what he was doing - however, it was usually not the doctors who cared or showed any kind of bed-side manner. She felt the needle go through her skin and thought maybe it wasn't such a bad idea to play along...

* * * * *

She wasn't sure how long she'd been asleep or how she'd made it back onto the couch. When she opened her eyes, she noted most of the light in the room came from a couple of candles. She looked down at the blankets wrapped around her and then at him sitting exposed to the cold at the other end of the couch. She tried to use her left hand on the back of the couch to hoist herself. The pain shot past the alcohol, and she flopped backward.

"Ouch," she cried.

"Ah, you're awake," he said standing. "I've got some soup warming on the wood burning stove." He put the soup into a mug and brought it to her. She reached for it and noticed her hand wrapped in torn sheets. She took the soup with her right hand and decided to drink it.

"How did the stitching go?" she asked trying to sit up.

"Once you passed out, it was fine. I didn't like all the moaning and groaning you did before that, though," he replied. "Maybe it's a good thing I'm not a doctor, or at least *your* doctor." The last part was barely audible. He sat down on the end of the couch by her feet.

"Here, I'll share with you," she said and kicked at the blankets so he could get under them. He smiled at her.

"It's a start," he replied.

Chapter Nine

She wasn't sure what jolted her awake first - the loud bang or the weight of something heavy falling on her. Struggling to move under the pressure - of what she wasn't quite sure yet, she tried to focus her eyes and gain some consciousness. It was a body! She struggled harder. Jack appeared, grabbed the dead weight by the back of a black skiing coat and pulled it off of her.

"Are you okay," he asked as he checked the man for a pulse. She scurried to the other side of the bed and tried to figure out where she was and how she had gotten there.

"Wha...what happened?" she stammered. "Who is that?"

"I don't know," Jack said. "I found him standing over you."

"So you take the 'shoot first, ask questions later' approach to law enforcement?" she practically screamed hysterically.

"He had a gun," Jack said and disappeared from the room. Her heart sank. What if these men weren't after him? What if they were there for her? She jumped out of bed, still in the oversized clothes and walked to the living room. Her head hurt, and her hand throbbed. "We have to go," he said. "Your clothes are dry - they've been by the fire. Change, and I'll pack the bags." He was scurrying around the room throwing things into the backpacks. This time, she didn't ask questions. She moved as quickly as she could with her injured hand. She was scared. She had thought she had been scared for the last two years - maybe she was and this was terror. Whatever it was, it was boiling in her. Jack called to her, "Come on Kristine. We have to go now!" She stopped dead in her tracks. Her heart sank farther, and her stomach leaped into her throat. Jack came to the door. "Come on."

"You know," she whispered with tears in her eyes.

"Know what? Come on. We have to go now," he said.

"You called me Kristine."

"No I didn't," he said with an anguished expression. "Why would I do that? Your name is Megan," he added unconvincingly. She shook her head. "Come on. I don't know if there was anyone with this guy." She swallowed hard, fought the tears and moved toward him. She took her backpack and followed him to the door. "Here. Take this," he said holding out a gun in his hand. She took it and put it into her coat. Her mind raced with questions, but her priority had to be getting out of the cabin and away from anyone who may have been with the dead man in the bedroom. "Stay out of sight."

Jack cautiously looked out the back window and then the front door, which was now open. Bolt cutters were lying in the snow next to the door, and a snowmobile was parked about five feet away. "I'm going to start the snowmobile. I'm not sure how far into the woods we'll get on the thing, but it's still faster than walking. Stay here. If you hear so much as a duck quack, go out the back and run like hell for the woods in a weaving pattern," he said. Still reeling from waking with a dead man on top of her and being called by her old name, she dumbly nodded without exactly knowing to what she had just agreed. "Hey," he nudged her. "I need you to snap out of it and concentrate on getting to the woods," he said. She nodded again. "Wait here, remember?" Not sure she could find her voice, she nodded again. He slowly walked out into the open area with his gun drawn and aimed at the woods. He moved in circles.

She studied the wooded surroundings. If there was anyone in the woods waiting for them, the person had a clean shot at him and would have taken it by now. She turned her attention to him and watched as he looked over the motorized sled. She heard the engine turn and rev once. She walked out onto the small concrete porch, which wasn't much bigger than a doormat. Jack drove up to the porch and held out a helmet, "Put it on," he said. She took the helmet and put it on. She climbed on the back of the vehicle and wrapped her arms around his waist. He started out slow and moved into the wooded area careful to dodge the low branches.

About 200 feet into the trees something hit the side of the snowmobile causing it to start smoking. Megan squeezed into Jack and heard him yell, "Hold on!" He pushed forward gaining speed. Megan, as if being hit with icy water, realized someone was shooting at them. She glanced from side to side hoping to see where the shot came from. She hadn't heard the first one, and she wondered if there were more. It was obvious even to her the snowmobile wouldn't hold out much longer. Jack tried to get as much out of it as he could. Megan couldn't see around Jack. He called to her, "Get ready to jump. Go to the right. On three. One, two, three."

The machine became air born as their bodies parted from it and fell to the right. Their snowmobile crashed into some trees and stopped running with a couple of sputters. They rolled when they landed. He drew the gun and scurried up the ledge of a snowdrift or hill. The rumble of another snowmobile came from behind them. Jack slid on his back down the hill and aimed the gun to the sky. The roar grew louder, and as the snow left the bottom of the stranger's vehicle, they caught sight of the man for the first time. Jack began to fire on the man, and the body separated from the machine. That snow mobile crashed near theirs in a thunderous bang. Megan laid on her back motionless, breathing heavy and aching. Jack slid to her and started to check her, "Can you move?" She nodded. "Are you hurt?" he asked touching her shoulder.

"I don't know," she whispered. "I think I'm in shock. Give me a minute," she added trying to regain strength and composure. He helped her sit up. "I think I'm okay." Her face said otherwise.

"You're hurt," he replied.

"I'm fine," she said irritated. She stood up and felt the cold air hit her wet backside, and it slapped her awake. She took a few steps forward. "I can't imagine why I'd be hurt. Let's see, so far I've fallen off the side of a mountain in a speeding van, been shot at and thrown off an air born snowmobile. I'm afraid to see what's next. You don't see any plane rides in our future, do you?" He stood up and watched her as she turned back toward him.

"Let's keep moving," he said and went to strip the body of its identification, money and whatever else he could find on it. This time she went with him. She found a cell phone lying by the body which she quickly picked up, turned off and put in her pocket without him noticing. She wasn't sure it worked, but between that and the gun she had with her, she felt a little safer. She watched him take the man's wallet and pat him down. "The gun must be around here somewhere," he said and squinted as he looked for the dark object in the white snow by the mound where they had landed. "Do you see it?"

She helped him look. She went to the wreckage of the man's snowmobile and kicked at the rubble. She found the gun and put it in her jacket with the phone. She wasn't sure why she didn't want Jack to know she had a spare gun on her, but she didn't. What he didn't know wouldn't hurt her, right? After all, he did call her Kristine. What else wasn't he telling her? "Do you think there are more?" she asked as she walked toward him. He looked up.

"Yeah, probably," he said and scanned the area around them.

"Then do you mind if we get going? I'm not in the mood to see anyone else die, especially us," she said and sighed in a sarcasm he must have found amusing by his smile. She was slightly taken aback by the sound of her tone and her words. Suddenly, she was sounding less and less like Megan and more and more like her old self. It felt like a release.

"Yeah, let's keep moving. We'll be safer if we stay in the wooded areas. We'll try to stay on the edge and find someplace to stay tonight," he took one more look around before they started picking their way through the woods again.

They walked for a few miles before she had enough courage to speak to him. "Jack?"

"Yeah," he said without breaking stride or looking at her.

"What happened back at the cabin?"

"What do you mean?"

"Let's start with why a dead guy fell on me. How did that happen?"

"Oh that," he said and slowed his pace slightly. "I went out to look around the woods and figure out where we were. While I was gone, I heard something coming from the direction of the cabin so I got back there as fast as I could. I saw the snowmobile and knew something wasn't right. Then when I saw him standing over you... Well, let's just say, I wasn't taking any chances."

She was still quiet while she tried to picture him - tried to get an idea of what thoughts ran through his head. "Have you killed many people before him?" He was quiet for a moment.

"Occupational hazard," he said quietly. "I don't think you ever get used to it."

"It doesn't seem to bother you, though," she said. "Not that I'm not grateful you showed up when you did," she added. He didn't reply. "What about the other thing?"

"The other thing?"

"You called me Kristine," she said. "Why was that?" He slowed down even more and finally stopped. She studied his face as he stared off into the forest. He took a deep breath and pulled off the backpack. He dug around in it and found two granola bars and a bottle of water, which he opened.

"I guess you should know it all," he said and motioned for her to sit down. He handed her a bar and the water. "My name really is Jack. I work for the FBI and was assigned to your case about a month ago." Her eyes dropped down to the ground. She wasn't sure why she was embarrassed, but she was. Maybe it was the intense sense of exposure she felt. She folded her arms as if to conceal herself just a little.

"Assigned to me... Go on," she said quietly.

"We have reason to believe the Rawlings family knows you're alive," he said. Her heart sputtered, and her eyes filled with tears. She nodded.

"So all this is about me." He nodded in return.

"Yeah," he confirmed. He put a hand out to touch her shoulder, but she turned away from him. She leaned against the base of a tree for support. "I tried to get you to tell me about your past on your own in the lodge."

"Damn," she murmured and stared at the bar.

"Listen, Megan...Kristine... Uh, I'm not sure what you want to be called," he said from behind her.

"Kristine died two years ago."

"You know, I think I've seen glimpses of her." Megan's head sprang up to face him.

"You don't know anything about me except what you've read in some file," she said so mad the tears spilled out of her eyes. "I'm a case number to you people. I'm someone you blame for getting myself into this mess and getting some agents killed. Don't pretend to give a crap about me." She leaned back against the tree and slid down it until she was sitting on the ground. "I'm not Kristine. Kristine didn't live her life looking over her shoulder, missing everyone she loved. I'm not Kristine, and now, if I get out of this alive, I probably won't even be Megan anymore. How is that fair? I go to prison and they walk around hunting me? Am I just supposed to keep peeling away layers of myself until there's nothing left?"

"I know it's not fair," he said trying to comfort her. "That's why I'm here to help you."

"Fair? It's so far beyond not fair," she laughed sarcastically. "I'm not free to walk down a street, live the life I wanted, fall in love, get married, have a baby. I'll never see my name on a Pulitzer Prize or a best sellers' list. What I do is not living - it's existing. You know what a real punishment would be? If I had to live in this hell for another 50 years," she said meaning every word. He watched her. "I can't do this anymore," she shook her head as she said the words.

"So you let them win?" he replied.

"Win? I can't fight a war with someone when the battle ground is this uneven," she said.

"Look," he said sitting beside her. "You're right about me not being able to know you from your file." She rolled her eyes. "It didn't tell me how feisty you are or how smart you are."

She thought about how this sounded like a lame pep-talk. If he broke out into the story of the little engine that could or an ant moving a rubber tree plant, she was going to smack him over the head with a tree branch.

"It also didn't discuss how much this had ruined your life. We don't tend to recognize that stuff. We think we're doing someone a huge favor by taking them out of their old life and giving them a new one," he said. "We pat ourselves on the back like we're heroes, because it would be too hard to admit the reason why we had to do it is the bad guys are still out there." She nodded subtly. "Oh man," he sighed. "There's something else you should really know." She raised her eyes.

"They didn't hurt anyone else? Is my family okay? What about Will?"

"Everyone else is fine," he said. "Okay. You have to listen to all of this - don't shut down." She agreed. "My last name isn't Hamilton. It's Rawlings."

"What!" she yelled nearly jumping to her feet.

"It's not what you think," he said following her. Her breathing was hard and fast. "My mom gave me to my aunt and uncle to be raised - that part of what I told you was true. By the time she got pregnant with me, she realized my father was a ruthless criminal. She could see my father's intentions of grooming my brother into being his clone. I joined the FBI to put my brother and father in jail, so my mother would be safe from them." He stopped and began again in a less panicked voice. "I was too late. I think he killed her."

Megan let this news sink into her brain. She remembered sitting in Will's apartment reading Carolyn Rawlings' obituary and thinking the same thing. She also remembered the note Carolyn had written to her. She wanted to protect her son - maybe the son was Jack. "I don't understand how a man like your father lets his son be raised by someone else. He seems too controlling for that."

"You're right. When my mother found out she was pregnant again, she stuck around as long as she could hide it. She told my father her sister was pregnant and confined to bed rest. She said she had to go help her until after the baby was born. Once my mom had me, she stayed for a few weeks and left. From what I know, my father had a lot of girlfriends so my mother's absence wasn't too much of a hardship for him. She came to see me a lot. When I was old enough to understand - well as much as a kid can understand this - my aunt, uncle and mom told me she was my mom. I didn't find out the rest of the story about how horrible my father is until I was much older - old enough to have started med school. My father didn't know about me until a mix up happened after my mother died. A lawyer accidentally sent Ralston some paperwork meant for me." Megan rubbed her head. This was a lot to digest and something she expected from a daytime drama - not from her own life.

"Wow," she said. "You're the son."

"What?"

"Your mom mentioned keeping a son and his family safe. I thought it was Ralston, but it didn't make sense. She was talking about keeping you and your aunt and uncle safe - unless you're married and/or have kids." Jack sat quietly looking as though he couldn't speak.

"I'm not married, and I don't have kids," he finally said. "She was protecting me until the day she died."

They sat in silence for a couple of minutes.

"So, how did you end up with me? Couldn't it be a conflict of interest or something?" she finally spoke. This snapped Jack out of whatever memory or thought he was having.

"My father wasn't too happy when he found out he had another son. Imagine his reaction when he found out I had decided to join the FBI for the soul purpose of putting him in jail for the rest of his life."

"So no father/son fishing trips? Sorry," she said silently cursing the timing of her sarcastic remark.

"Not exactly. When he finally made contact, I was still mourning the loss of my mother. I swore I'd either put him away for the rest of his life for killing her or kill him myself."

"I probably shouldn't bring this up, but don't you think killing comes a little too easily to you Rawlings?"

"I didn't mean it literally… Well, maybe I did. I don't know. I was just so pissed off."

"That still doesn't tell me how you ended up with my case," she said settled enough to take a bite of her breakfast.

"I was going through the evidence against my family. I saw your testimony to the original agents that my mother had been in contact with you. I went to the director and asked for you. I guess I thought if I couldn't save her from them, I could save you."

"I guess that makes sense," she said. "So now what?"

"Now we get off this mountain and get you stashed away again," he said.

"Oh no. I'm not doing another relocation. If I get off this mountain, I'm going back to my old life. Screw this hiding thing," she said.

"You might as well walk around with a bull's eye on your back," he said. "You're a survivor. Don't let them get you."

"I don't want to just survive. I want to breathe again," she said.

"You won't be able to do it from your grave. We have to get moving," he said. She looked up at him with her green eyes so tired and soft.

"If it happens, at least I would have peace," she said swallowing hard and feeling the lump in her throat again.

"Let's go. We'll find peace later. Right now, I'd settle for a way off this mountain," he said. "Come on. We can do this. We stay here, and we're both going to die. And I'm not ready for that. This would make a great story, but you're going to have to live to write it."

"Before we go, let's get something straight," she said mustering her courage and putting the wrapper of the bar in her coat pocket. "I'm not sure whether I believe you. If you're truly from the FBI, why are you alone? Why isn't this mountain crawling with agents - or at least one or two more? From what I've seen, the FBI never does anything this simplified. Unfortunately, I think I have a better chance of getting off this mountain with you than without you. So for now, we're sticking together."

He nodded quietly.

Chapter Ten

They walked in silence. She was still feeling hungry and tired. Still, all those hours on the treadmill had made her legs stronger than his, and she could tell he was tiring faster than she was. Her mind jumped from scene to scene. If the Rawlings' organization knew she was alive, did her family? Did Will? If not, could she call them now? She wondered what she would say to them - it's not every day someone gets a call from a dead person. If she was able to reclaim her life, would she go back to work as a reporter? Excitement grew in the pit of her stomach. What if she could resume her old life as if none of this had happened? Would Will still want her? The image of him happy with someone else - maybe his wife and daughters - crept into her thoughts. Home Wrecker wasn't exactly a label she wanted attached to her. If she could resume her life, it wouldn't be as if her apartment was waiting for her. Her clothes were gone, her desk at the office was occupied by someone else - of course sitting somewhere away from Burt Newman had its appeal - she wasn't sure if she could even locate everyone. This was seriously jumping ahead of herself. She wasn't even assured of getting off the mountain alive much less being able to live in the open as Kristine Larkin again. Man, her hand hurt.

"Hey, I have to go to the bathroom," she said and stopped. He stopped and looked around.

"Go ahead, I'll wait here," he sat down and leaned up against a tree. She moved to the left through some trees, and when she was what she considered a safe distance, she took out the phone and turned it on. She tried to remember Will's phone number at the office. She looked at the numbers and began to dial. She stopped. What if they knew she called him?

He was the one person in the world who she could trust, count on, and who may actually have the contacts to be able to help her, and she couldn't call him. She turned the phone off and put it away. Leaning her head back so the tears wouldn't fall down her cheeks, she told herself she wasn't allowed to cry. She began to walk back toward Jack. An unfamiliar voice startled her. She ducked behind a tree and looked out in the direction of a scuffle. Jack was fighting with a man. She watched for a moment and then pulled out one of the guns she had stashed inside her coat. She moved swiftly but quietly between trees. Finally, the fighting stopped. Jack was standing with his hands in the air and was staring at a gun being pointed at him.

"Where is she, Jack?" the other man demanded angrily.

"She died in the van wreck," Jack said.

"You should know better than to lie to me," the man hissed back. Megan tried to aim the gun. She had learned to use a gun before she was hidden away in her new life, but she hadn't fired one in years. At this point, even a distraction would help. She blinked several times. Why was she worried about hitting Jack? She steadied her hand. He had just lied about whether she was alive. She didn't think she had time to debate his motives so she took a deep breath and squeezed the trigger.

The bullet lodged in the stranger's side, and he fell to the ground. Jack pulled his gun from his jacket and fired repeatedly on the man. Jack looked up in the direction where she was standing. She emerged from her hiding place and stared at the dead man on the ground.

"Did I kill him?" she asked in shock. She thought she had valued human life too much to ever take one unless she was in danger. Did this make her an animal on equal playing ground as a Rawlings?

"No, I think you got him in the lung," Jack said as he again stripped the body of its belongings. She looked at the gun in her hand. "There's another guy out looking for you, come on." As they began to go forward through the woods another gunshot rang out. He took her hand, and they began running. They leaped over fallen branches, got scratched by low limbs and scrambled through some thick brush. Flashes of green and white passed by her eyes, and all she could focus on was Jack's back.

They came to a slope and slid down it feet first. He looked up at the top of the slope. There was no one there…yet. They scrambled to their feet and headed for the thick brush, to their right. Once into the cover of the denser woods, he stopped. He pulled her behind a large evergreen and put his finger to his lips in a motion that let her know she should be quiet. They crouched, and he pushed her into the branches. He maneuvered onto his stomach and did what looked like an army crawl using only his arms to pull him under the lowest lying branches. She tried to control her breathing so she would not be heard. After what seemed like an eternity, a single shot was fired and the branches clawed at her as they moved. Jack was moving out of his position. His hand reached into the needles and pulled her out. She didn't say a word as she watched him pick the body clean of its wallet and gun. Before either of them had caught their breath, they were off again. It would be much harder to track them through this area because the snow was unable to pile up on the ground as it had in the wide open or less dense areas. When the sun began to set, they stopped to take a break.

"We have to find someplace to stay tonight," Megan huffed. Her legs hurt, her head pounded, her hand throbbed. Had she been in less intense circumstances, she would have collapsed long ago.

"We'll be all right," he said seemingly as much to reassure

himself as he said it for her.

"We'll freeze. We can't build a fire. We need someplace to stay," she said.

"You're right. If we can't sleep, we'll have to keep moving," he stood up. She could see the fatigue on his face. Neither of them would make it until morning without some rest. Still, they had nowhere to go. He pulled out a map from his jacket, which he had taken off the last man who made the mistake of tracking them. She looked up at him and watched his movements carefully. Trusting someone wasn't an easy thing for her to do. Following her gut and listening to her head over her heart was easy. Unfortunately, nothing was sending her a clear signal, well except for an occasional hormone. Jack even looked handsome with pine needles in his hair, unshaven, dirt on his cheek and crusty scabs on his forehead. He was tough and serious. But when he looked at her, he seemed all soft and warm. She tried to clear her head. Puppies were soft and warm. Men claiming to be FBI agents and part of a family, whose purpose in life is to hunt you, are not. She watched him study the map.

"That would help a lot more if it came with a 'You are Here' indicator on it," she wise-cracked knowing he was just as lost as she was.

"I can figure this out," he looked around the sky. "We're heading down the mountain. That has to mean something." He looked back at the map and up again at the sky.

"Good God, let me at least help you," she said standing. She felt the blood rush to her head and felt faint. Her face went from flushed warmth to ghostly white. He stepped to her and took her arm.

"Sit down," he said. Crap, she thought. There was that puppy dog warmth she was trying to convince herself didn't exist. He touched her uninjured hand and took her pulse. He moved his fingers around her wrist. "I'm having a problem getting a good spot. Let me check your neck." Megan sat there motionless staring at him. He brushed her hair away from the neck of her coat and reached two fingers into her turtleneck. His hands were cold on her neck. She swallowed hard. She closed her eyes in an effort to block out his face and his touch. All that managed to do was send her thoughts flying into directions that made her eyelids pop open.

"I'm fine," she insisted and pulled his hand away from her bare neck. She stood - more slowly this time - and felt steady on her feet. She took the map out of his other hand. "Okay, we started out here," she said and located the lodge on the map. "About here is where you drove us off the cliff," she said and looked up to catch his crinkled brow and deep gaze as he focused on her. She smirked at him and looked back at the map. She was really trying not to show any interest in him. "If we traveled an average of two and a half miles an hour over the last two days during the daylight hours, we should be somewhere in here," she said making a circle on the map with her finger.

He grinned and said, "Well, you've just narrowed it down to a 20 mile radius." He took the map from her and began his squinted look around the woods. He looked at the map again.

"And you can do better, Columbus?" she asked snidely.

"Columbus found America by mistake. Let's go this way," he said and pointed toward their left.

"On what are you basing this decision?" she asked as he started walking. She followed him, because she didn't have a better idea.

"Call it male intuition," he said moving ahead.

"Comforting," she said. He ignored the comment.

It was getting darker. They walked for almost two hours as dusk turned into night. He glanced at the map and eventually had to pull out the flashlight from his bag. Just as Megan was beginning to think they would have to walk through the night, they came to the edge of the woods. Her first urge was to run out, find a cheeseburger and a bed, and sleep for three days straight. He put out his arm to stop her.

"Stay here," he said. "I'll be back." At this point, she was so tired she didn't care if he left her there all night. She slumped against a tree and closed her eyes. "Hey," he said as he gently shook her by the shoulders. "Don't fall asleep. It's too cold. You have to stay awake until I get back." She nodded. He took a good look at her and carefully moved out of the woods.

* * * * *

The sound of breaking tree limbs and crunching snow shook Megan out of a light sleep. She wasn't sure how she ended up on the ground, when it happened or how long she had been there.

"Are you okay?" Jack asked as he knelt beside her.

"Yeah," she replied trying to stand. "Just resting my eyes. What did you find?"

"There's a motel down the street about a mile. I found a couple of kids leaving a room and convinced them to give me the key." She hesitated.

"How did you do that?" she asked not sure she really wanted to know.

"Two hundred bucks," he said as he started for the tree line. She sighed in relief. It was one thing when you shot someone who wanted to shoot you. It was a different story when you shot someone for being in the wrong place at the wrong time. "I'm not going to kill a couple kids for a not-so-slightly used motel room, Megan," he said sounding disappointed in her.

"I'm just not sure where you draw that line," she said before she could think about her comment. He ignored it.

"We'll stay along the tree line until we get closer," he said. The temperature had dropped, she thought. Although never being one for much spiritual speculation, she wondered about the coincidence of finding warm places two nights in a row. The cynic's voice returned and reminded her of the living hell the last two years of her life had been. Still, what if everything happened for a reason, she thought? What if that which does not kill us really does make us stronger? Chasing the thoughts from her mind, she decided to revisit this debate if she survived this latest predicament.

"Jack?"

"Yeah."

"Are we almost there?"

"Just a little farther."

"Jack?"

"Yeah."

"I think I'm going to fall down," she had stopped and was swaying like a palm tree against a hurricane. He turned and grabbed her as her legs started to buckle under her. She tried not to lose consciousness. "I'm so sorry," she whispered.

"It's okay," he said. He tried to lift her.

"No. You can't carry me," she said. "You're about to fall over, too."

"I'm okay," he said.

"Just let me lean a little until we get there. Okay?" He put her arm around his neck and his arm around her waist to help support her.

"We're almost there," he said. "You've lost too much blood."

"This is better," she said and mustered strength to walk farther.

"You fell asleep while I was gone, didn't you?" he asked in a fatherly tone.

"Can we debate my sleep patterns later? It's taking all I have to move right now," she said.

Just as she was convinced she may collapse, the hotel came into sight. The light at the end of the tunnel, or tree line, gave her a mental and maybe even physical boost.

"Can you make it," he asked.

"Yeah."

Jack helped Megan out of the woods, across a small patch of snow onto the parking lot, past a dumpster so frozen it forgot to smell and up a flight of stairs to the second level of the two story motel.

"We're here," he said. He unlocked and opened the door and flipped on the light without letting go of Megan's waist. The double bed was unmade and empty condom wrappers and beer cans littered the floor.

"Looks like we missed the party," she said. The warmth from the room hit her with such force she felt sick to her stomach for a moment.

"Yeah. I have a feeling this place rents by the hour," he replied helping her remove her backpack and sit in one of the two chairs separated by a round table in front of the window. He went to the bed and separated the flat sheet from the blanket. He removed the fitted sheet and replaced it with the flat sheet, tucking it between the mattress and box spring. "It's probably not the most sanitary environment, but it's going to have to do."

"I'm too exhausted to care," she said trying to stand.

"Let me help you," he said. He helped her take off her coat. "Uh, I'll wait in the bathroom while you get out of the wet clothes and under the covers." She nodded.

"Jack?" she said in a soft voice cloaked in pain and

exhaustion. He came out of the bathroom. "I can't do it," she said. "My fingers are so cold and my left hand really hurts."

"It's okay. I'll help you," he said.

"I don't want you to help me," she began to cry. "I want to go home. I'm scared." He walked to her and put his arms around her. After a moment, she pushed him away. "Just help me, please so I can get in bed and get warm." He felt so good, but she still wasn't sure about him. Was it him or was it just the last name that made her afraid to trust him completely? He helped her out of her shoes, pulled off her sweatshirt and jeans. She got into the bed as he folded the blanket in two so it was doubled over her.

* * * * *

Megan felt something nudge her gently on the shoulder. She sighed and slowly opened her eyes. "I'm so tired," she whispered. Jack was sitting along side her on the bed.

"I know. I didn't want to wake you, but I really need to look at you. You took a hard fall from the snowmobile this morning. I got some stuff to fix you up, see?" he asked and looked toward the nightstand where there were bandages, peroxide, pain relievers and a glass of water. "The first thing we need to do is clean you up." He stood up, and she struggled to the edge of the bed. "I'll help you, here," he said and offered her his hand. She took it, and he pulled her up. He put his arm around her waist and helped her into the bathroom. She leaned against the door frame. He turned on the water in the tub and asked her, "Shower or bath?"

"Shower," she said and started trying to tug at the long-john shirt she wore. He took the little bottle of shampoo and the tiny bar of soap from the counter top. He then took a wash cloth and placed them all within easy reach in the shower. She could feel him watching her to see if she needed more help. As much as she did, she wasn't going to let him take off all of her clothes. "Can you just unhook my bra? I think it would take both my hands." His now warm, chapped hands reached under her shirt, and she could swear she felt his breath on her neck. She closed her eyes and felt the release when the hooks were undone. "I've got it from here," she said without turning. He stood still for a few seconds.

"Are you sure? It sounds lame, but I *was* going to be a doctor. You don't have anything I haven't seen."

"Well, you weren't going to be *my* doctor. I can finish undressing myself."

"Okay, I'll be outside if you need me," he said and headed toward the door.

"You can leave the door open a little, just in case." She knew she was weak and wasn't sure how long she could hold herself up.

He left, and she removed the rest of her clothing, unwrapped her bandaged hand and pulled the stopper to turn on the shower head. She tried to carefully wash her left hand and saw the blood in the water below her. She washed her hair and the rest of her body as best she could one handed and turned off the shower. Losing that much blood was probably making her more tired and weaker than she should be, she thought.

"Are you all right?" Jack called from the bedroom.

"Yeah," she said and stepped from the tub. She rinsed her delicates in the sink and hung them on the towel rack. It didn't even occur to her that Jack may use the bathroom and see them. She gingerly picked up her clothes and yelled to Jack, "Do you have anything I can put on?" He went to his bag and pulled out a flannel shirt. He walked to the bathroom door, and she met him holding a towel in front of her. "Thanks," she said and took the clothes.

"There's a coin laundry down the hall. If you give me your clothes, I'll take them down and run them through the washer and dryer."

"I'll bring them out," she said and didn't move from the door.

"Sure," he said and retreated back to the side of the bed. She combed her hair with the fingers on her right hand. Using the hair dryer on the wall, she dried her hair until it was only slightly damp. She took her clothes from the counter and left the bathroom.

"Just put the clothes on the dresser, and I'll take them down," he said. "How do you feel?" he asked.

"Better. My hand is pretty bad, though. It's been bleeding off and on all day, and it started again in the shower." She sat down on the bed where she had been sleeping. He pulled one of the yellow velour covered chairs over to the edge of the bed and sat down.

"Let me see," he said and reached for her hand. He looked at it and grabbed for the peroxide and the bag of cotton balls he had bought. "I got some food and some drinks," he said and began to apply the peroxide to her wound. She cringed and wiggled from the sight of the peroxide bubbling. She looked up at the ceiling as tears formed in her eyes. Her hand hurt more than she thought she could handle.

"I'm sorry, but I have to do this," he said.

"I know," she said and grabbed at a pillow with her other hand.

"I need to do more stitching," he said and waited - maybe to hear an approval or protest.

"Do what you have to," she said knowing she couldn't keep bleeding like this. To take her mind off what was happen to her hand, she began to run through all the reasons why she shouldn't and should trust him. He had had plenty of chances to kill her, and he had come back to the woods for her. He could have left her. It would have been much easier for him to travel by himself and leave her there. She looked at him long enough to see him trying to thread a needle. "I can't watch this," she said and laid down on the bed, her hand still outstretched. She also didn't want him to see her crying. She pressed her toes against the headboard.

It took him what seemed like hours to finish her hand. He cleaned it again and wrapped it up with gauze and bandages. "Your hand's finished. I'd like to check the rest of you out," he said noticing the cuts and bruises all over her face, legs and arms.

"Do whatever you have to," she said her voice cracked and tears rolled down her eyes to the pillow.

He stood over her. He gently pushed on her abdomen, "Does this hurt?"

"No," she said and felt his hands move around her as he kept asking the question. She jumped when he felt her rib area.

"You may have some broken ribs," he said. "Are you having trouble breathing?"

"I don't think so. It just hurts a little," she said. He wet another cotton ball with peroxide and dabbed at her arms, legs and face. The other wounds were painful, but compared to what she felt in her hand, it barely registered to her.

"Can you eat something?" he asked when he was finished. She opened her eyes and heard him rustling through the bags behind her. "I got peanut butter and some chips. It's not filet mignon, but they didn't have much of a selection," he said.

"It's fine. When did you go to the store?" she asked as she turned herself around in the bed and leaned against the headboard.

"While you were sleeping," he said. She watched him as

he prepared her sandwich.

"Did anyone say anything about the way you look?"

"I told the cashier I had a skiing mishap," he said as he put the sandwich together.

"It was a woman, wasn't it?" she asked with a smile as she took the sandwich.

"What?"

"The cashier."

"Yes."

"Yeah. That's what I thought," she said smiling and took a bite of the sandwich. He brought her a small carton of milk and a bag of chips.

"Why does it matter?" he asked with a grin that revealed he knew exactly what she was going to say.

"Because you could sell a spot on Mt. Rushmore to some women," she said.

"Oh yeah?" he replied with a touch of satisfaction as he made himself a sandwich.

"I didn't say that was necessarily a good thing," she said.

"Why do you say that?" He turned to take a curious look at her.

"Because it makes smart women not trust you," she said being honest. He turned with his sandwich, chips and milk and went to the chair and table next to the bed.

"You don't trust me?" She thought for a second before she answered him.

"Not completely. No," she said taking another bite of her sandwich.

"You can, you know," he said starting his sandwich.

"It's not that I don't want to, but," she said and stopped for a moment before continuing. "But, you're too smooth. And, to be honest, you didn't start off well with all the lying."

"It's not exactly like I could walk up to you in the middle

of your class and say, 'Hi, I'm the son of the man trying to kill you, and he knows you're alive. I'm here to help you.' Now, can I?"

"In my classroom?" she asked with a sick feeling in the pit of her stomach. "How long have you been following me?" She put the remaining part of her sandwich on her leg.

"Awhile," he said. "Hey, how's the pain in your hand? I bought something for the pain. Do you need some?"

"You changed the subject. And for the record, this is a huge gash in my hand, not pre-menstrual cramps. How long have you been following me?" Jack sighed.

"It's more like keeping an eye on you."

"What's the difference?"

"Watching you sounds creepy. Watching you requires a restraining order. What I was doing was for your protection."

"How long," she demanded.

"About a month - give or take a couple of days," he said quickly stuffing more sandwich in his mouth.

"A month!?" she replied in disbelief. He nodded. "And no one bothered to tell me I was in danger? What about the kids at the school? Did anyone care what could have happened to them?"

"You were on a need to know basis," he said. "My bosses didn't think you needed to know."

"You people make me sick. You think you can just screw with people for the fun of it. I didn't need to know, is that right? Some lunatic from your gene pool is out there trying to kill me, and I didn't need to know that? Go to hell. All of you." She was standing now - the uneaten portion of her sandwich on the floor. "I'm getting out of here." She went to pack the backpack on the dresser, but before she could put anything in it, she noticed a bullet hole. Jack was now standing next to her. She put her finger through the hole.

"Go lie down before you start bleeding again," he said taking the backpack. She looked up at him.

"Is this a…?" she blinked. He nodded. "Is it the one I was wearing?" He nodded again.

"Go lie down," he said and put the backpack on the dresser.

"Why didn't the bullet hit me?" she asked standing at the dresser staring at the hole.

"Because it hit a can of soup I packed in the cabin," he said taking her by the arm and leading her back to the bed. She swallowed hard and let him guide her back to the bed. She sat down and stared at the sandwich on the floor. He picked up the sandwich and tossed it into the garbage. Then he sat in the chair across from her. "Look, it didn't hit you. You're okay." He put his hands on her legs. "You're okay," he said again slower.

"Is this what you call okay?"

"Relatively speaking," he said. "It's not the best situation, but you're here to fight another day."

"Great. Prolong the inevitable," she said feeling weaker by the second.

"Not if I can help it," he said. He used his hand to lift her chin and her eyes to him then returned it to her leg. "We've already come this far. We can do this."

"Do what? Run every day for the rest of our lives dodging bullets with backpacks packed with soup cans?" she said. "That sounds fun," she added with a sarcastic grunt.

"There's a way out of this, I promise. We just have to get you to a safe house," he said rubbing her legs. She looked down at his hands and then up at him with a raised eyebrow. He removed his hands quickly. "Sorry."

"I need to think," she said and sat back against the headboard again. After about a half hour of sitting in silence, she looked over at him. He looked awful in a really melt your heart kind of way. "What about you?"

"Huh?" he said looking surprised by the sound of her voice.

"Are you okay?" she asked surprised by the fact she really did care.

"I'm fine," he said. She didn't know if she believed him. He stood up. "I'm going to take a shower and then wash our clothes."

"I'll start the clothes while you're in the shower," she said.

"No. You stay hidden. I'm more used to moving without being seen." She shrugged and pulled the blanket over her.

He took another flannel shirt and a pair of long johns from the backpack and walked toward the bathroom.

"Hey! How come you get the long johns?" she said in protest.

"Because you have the better legs," he said as he disappeared. For the next 10 minutes she found herself chasing images of him in the next room under the running water from her mind. She tried to act like she was sleeping when he came out of the bathroom.

"I know you're wake," he said.

"How do you know I'm awake?" she asked lifting one eye lid.

"Because I could hear you mumbling to yourself before I opened the door," he said.

"What did I say?" she asked mildly worried.

"I don't know exactly. Sounded like, 'stop it' or something," he said running his fingers through his hair to tame it.

"I could have been talking in my sleep," she said.

"But you weren't," he said gathering their clothes. He went back into the bathroom and came out carrying an ice bucket and the undergarments she had hung on the towel rack. She felt embarrassed and excited by the fact he had them in his hands. "Do you want me to throw these in with the rest," he said as if there was nothing to it.

"Uh, I guess, yeah," she answered. He seemed to grin at her discomfort.

"Want to carry around my boxers for while so we'll be even?" he asked in a playful tone. She smiled, shook her head and let out a sigh that could have been a laugh. "I'll be right back." She nodded, and he added, "Don't open the door for anybody. I have the key." He opened the door and peeked down the hallways and in the direction of the parking lot.

It didn't take him long to return, and she was relieved to hear his key jiggle in the lock. For the first time in two days she was starting to feel safer. He came in and put the bucket down on the dresser. He went to the bathroom, grabbed a towel and wrapped some ice in it. He walked to her and handed her the ice pack. "Here, put this on your hand." She tried to keep her eyes from wondering to the long johns, but it was a struggle she wasn't winning.

"Why don't you rest for awhile?" she asked watching him. "You have to be exhausted."

"If I do, I won't get back up," he said. "I have to switch the laundry to the dryer in half an hour."

"Okay," she said sounding disappointed and thought she may have caught a glimpse of a grin on his face as he moved around the room organizing their belongings. "Want me to stay up with you?" He turned out the lights - all except the bathroom, he just closed the door partially so they could use it as a nightlight.

"No. You get some sleep."

"You can sleep in the bed when the clothes are finished," she said. She decided it sounded too much like an invitation for more. "I'll build a barrier with the blanket," she added trying not to sound like a woman who had just fantasized about him in the shower for 10 minutes.

"Thanks," he said and sat down in the chair. "You go to sleep, and I'll take the ice off your hand in a couple of minutes."

"Okay," she said and nestled into the bed. She closed her eyes and managed one more peek at him as if to reassure herself he was there. "Goodnight," she murmured and fell asleep.

Chapter Eleven

She was jolted awake by the sounds of her own dreams. Jack was sleeping in the chair across from her, but she must have done something to wake him.

"Are you okay?" he asked getting out of the chair and standing over her. "It's just a dream."

"Unfortunately, it wasn't just a dream," she said rubbing her eyes with her right hand.

"Well, hopefully it will be over soon," he said stretching.

"Jack? Why won't they just leave me alone?"

"I don't know. I don't understand it, and I share DNA with them. You put Ralston in prison, and I don't think daddy dearest is thrilled about his first born being some guy's 'special friend.' You did something to them, and now they do something to you."

"But, I lost everything. I lost my family, my job, my home, my friends, an amazing man - even who I was. Why wasn't that enough?"

"I guess the way they see it, you threaten everything they have and feel they earned." She was quiet as she remembered everything that lead up to that horrid day in the restaurant.

"What did they tell you?" she asked wondering how much he knew of her story.

"Who?" he asked.

"The FBI. About me."

"Oh, the usual," he replied in a tentative voice. "Pretty much everything there was to know actually."

"Can I tell you about me?" she asked unsure whether he was even interested in her story. Still, she wanted him to know she was a person with feelings - not just a name on paper.

"Yeah, I'd like that," he said. He pulled the chair a little closer to her. She rolled onto her side in the bed and waited for him to get settled.

"My name was Kristine Larkin. I grew up wanting to be somebody special. I went to a small college and landed the most incredible job, because the editor liked me in a not-so-professional kind of way. Everyone knew it, but I didn't let it stop me from becoming the most aggressive reporter the paper had. I was going to change the world, but not because I wanted to make it a better place. I wanted to change it so people would respect me, want to come up to me on the street and shake my hand. I wanted to be rich and famous and go on talk shows telling everyone about how I helped to clean up the world and make it safe for their children just because I was a hell of a person. My boss left his wife for the image of the woman I wanted him to see - not who I really was. It took endless nights sitting alone in an apartment living someone else's life for me to see all this clearly."

He was still and listened as she continued. "Then one day, I got in over my head. I agreed to meet a man from the FBI at a restaurant. He took a bullet meant for me. In fact, I'm the only one who survived that day. You know how? I crawled over dead people, hid behind the bar and smeared myself with another man's blood. When your family came in looking for signs of life," she trailed off and took a deep breath. "I thought I was dead. I was so thankful to be alive. I thought I would pick right back up where I left off. I identified the man with the gun as your brother. And then everything changed. I went back to being nobody who had to remain nobody for the rest of her life to stay alive.

"Ambition almost killed me, and it was the only thing I knew how to do. So then I didn't feel so lucky anymore. I sat up at night wishing someone would have noticed I was alive and shot me. Now, when I see a little old lady in the grocery store parking lot I help her put her bags in her car, because I can't change the world anymore. The only thing I could change was me. That's how I got here, Jack - because I was a piece of shit person. Now that I know enough to be a better one, I'll spend the rest of my life running."

"You were never a bad person. You were young. Everyone's self-absorbed when they're young," he said.

"It's so weird how your priorities change when your life is turned upside down," she said wiping a runaway tear from her cheek. "I never thought that marriage and kids and a house with a little white picket fence in suburbia were important. I thought that was for simpletons," she laughed at her stupidity. "Now that I want the husband, two kids, a dog and a spot on the PTA, I can't have it. Do you think that's justice? Because I'm wondering if I didn't get exactly what I deserve." He got out of his chair and knelt before her. He brushed her hair off of her face and caught a tear with his thumb before it hit her pillow. "I'm not going to get a second chance, am I?"

"Listen to me," he said in a tender, yet strong voice. "We're going to get out of this. I don't know how yet but when we do, you're going to be able to do everything you've ever wanted and more. I swear to you. I owe you that much." She smiled and felt her heart beat a little faster. She looked into his brown eyes and thought she saw guilt. "You're so...," he whispered and then suddenly stood and walked toward the other side of the room. She saw their clothes folded on the dresser. He dipped a glass in the ice bucket and then took a drink.

"How did you get here?" she asked. He turned and walked back to his chair.

"Wow, talk about long stories," he looked down at the glass in his hand. "I'll give you the short version. My mother hid me from my father. When I finally figured out just how awful the truth was about him, I felt I had to do something about it. I was so close to practicing medicine. My mother would have been proud of me. It broke her heart when I joined the FBI. She understood it, but she worried about me until the day she died," he cleared his throat. "She didn't like what my father did or who he was, but I think it hurt her to know we were pitted against each other. She wanted me to save the world by finding a cure for cancer, not by sending my father to prison."

"You still would have been helping people if you had become a doctor. You could have saved all the people your family shot," she said only half jokingly. He grinned slightly and took a drink of water.

"I'll be happy if I can just save you," he said. "Now, go to sleep. I want to get out of here early tomorrow."

* * * * *

The sound of a car ignition brought the sleeping Megan into a groggy, half-awake state. She glanced at the window. No more light shined through the bottom of the curtains than had hours ago when she fell asleep. Still dark, she thought. She looked over at Jack sitting in the chair. His chin rested on his chest, his mouth hung partially open. She was suddenly thankful. Thankful for the bathroom light he had left on over night. Thankful she wasn't alone. Even thankful for the pain in her left hand, because it meant she was alive.

She studied him. He was fit - not overly muscular but strong. His arms were crossed, fingers hidden beneath his biceps. She smiled as she pictured him as a child, tiny little fingers clutching his favorite stuffed animal - she decided it was a bear. Its ear torn from being used as a handle when he carried it, an eye ready to fall off and a worn nose.

The clicking from the heat register brought her back. She blinked hard. Taking a deep breath, inhaling the hotel smell, she quietly sat up and removed the covers. She noticed an extra blanket over her and looked back at the sleeping stranger. She knew he had watched her. Watched her sleep and maybe even noticed a shiver. She couldn't remember if she had been cold. She began to rise and the bed springs sighed. Jack's eyes sprang open as he shot upright in the chair reaching for a gun on the table next to him.

"It's just me," she whispered. He relaxed. "I'm sorry." He hunched in the chair and rubbed the back of his neck. He looked up at her. She stood over him, and he cleared his throat.

"Where are you going?"

"Bathroom. It's still night. Why don't you take the bed for awhile?"

"I'm fine," he said and leaned back in the chair.

"Okay. Thanks for the blanket," she said. He just looked at her. She smiled and went toward the light of the bathroom.

Chapter Twelve

Megan didn't jump when she felt the hand on her shoulder. Maybe she was still too tired to care whether the person touching her was a good guy or a bad guy, or maybe she had found a little comfort. She rolled from her side onto her back and raised her eyes. In a raspy voice she said, "What time is it?"

"About 5:30," he said as he went to the ice bucket to get the juice he had stored there last night. He shook one, opened it and took it to her. "Here," he said, and she sat up in the bed. He took another, shook it and opened it. He turned around to her and rested against the dresser.

"You can come over here and sit down if you want," she said and moved her stretched out legs into a cross-legged position under the blanket. He looked at her without expression. "I promise I won't bite or shoot you or anything like that," she said. He walked over and sat on the edge of the bed.

"I think I know how I can get your life back for you," he said.

"How?" she asked and sat up a little more with an anxious curiosity.

"I'm going to my father's. He has to keep some sort of records in the house. We've never been able to get a search warrant for the house. Unfortunately, whatever I find will not be admissible in court without a search warrant."

"Funny, it sounds more like suicide than a plan," she said disappointed in his idea.

"It's the only way you won't have to go back into the program. Even if you do, they won't give up," he said looking down at his juice. They were quiet for a moment while they thought about their plight.

"I think you're right," she said gaining some confidence in the plan. "The last thing they would expect is for us to go to them. If we can at least get some evidence, we could blackmail them into letting us live."

"There's no 'we' in this plan. I'm going to get you to a safe house and then go," he said with conviction. "There's probably one other thing you should know," he said.

"What," she asked suspiciously.

"While I do work for the FBI, I was pulled from your case when they found out Rawlings was my father. I'm on administrative leave for disobeying orders."

"What orders did you disobey?"

"I was ordered to stay off the case and away from you," he said. "I hacked into computer files to find you." Something about this statement made her uneasy. Still, she was stuck on the side of a mountain hurt, and he was the closest thing to help she had.

"So basically, you're on your own if you go into the Rawlings house? No backup?" she said.

"No."

"Well, then I'd say you need me," she said. She wasn't sure why she was so willing to put herself in danger again. Still, she thought, this would make an amazing story. The thought of sitting in a safe house again with agents being nasty to her didn't sound very appealing - it was horrible the first time around. She'd rather be free to dodge bullets than be locked up in a house. "I can be your lookout or something. I can quack like a duck or hoot like an owl if someone's coming," she said.

"I think you've watched too many cartoons. We don't hoot like owls," he said grinning.

"You know what I mean. I'm in the mood to take back my

life. Are you with me or not?" she asked removing the blanket and standing.

"With you? It's my plan," he said smiling. "Now, let's get ready to go before it gets any later." He ran his eyes from her face down her body to her legs. She felt uncomfortable at the thought that the flannel shirt was the only thing that separated her skin from his eyes. She pulled down the shirt and then folded her arms in front of her.

"I'll get ready," she said and turned to the shelter of the light, grabbing her clothes from the dresser on her way. She closed the door behind her and locked it. She laid her clothes on the counter next to the sink and used her fingers to comb her hair. "To have the luxury of a toothbrush." she thought out loud. She rinsed her mouth and face with water and put on her clothes.

Opening the door slowly, she said, "Are you decent?"

"Yeah," he said with sleep still in his throat. She walked out of the bathroom and saw him standing at the dresser. He had put on his jeans and tucked a T-shirt into them. She caught sight of his hair and tried not to laugh. The night air hadn't been kind to the contrasting strands of short hair - spreading them in every direction. "What's so funny?"

"Your hair," she said and laughed out loud. He looked in the mirror and tried to flatten it with his hand. Now she was out of control, nearly doubled over. The realization that it wasn't that funny couldn't stop her. The sound of her laughter was contagious. He began laughing as he turned to watch her. She sat on the edge of the bed and flopped backwards. Laugh tears rushed from her eyes, and she heard him snort through the joy. She raised a finger to try to point at him before slapping it down on the bed. Stress made people react in very weird ways, she thought.

Suddenly a door, maybe as close as next door, slammed.

They moved so quickly toward each other in silence that their bodies met with force. He wrapped his arms around her and put his body between her and the door.

"It's just a door," she whispered with her arms drawn into her body. He removed his arms from around her and pushed her toward the bathroom.

"Probably. I want to look, though. Take this and wait in the bathroom," he said and handed her a gun. She walked toward the bathroom, and as she reached the door, she turned and saw him looking through the peephole in the door. Courage climbed from her stomach and took over her. She moved back to the sleeping area with quiet confidence. Jack had moved to the side of the window and peeked out through the curtain.

He saw her and raised a finger to his lips. She went to the peephole and looked out. She saw two men walk past the door and then looked at Jack in shock. He nodded his head slightly, and she moved to the other side of the curtain. He moved also to get a better look.

There were three men standing at the end of the hall. Two were rather tall. The third man seemed to be giving instructions. He was shorter than the other two and looked slightly out of shape, but it was hard to tell with only a hall light and a long black leather coat hanging from him. His hair was dark, curly and thinning on the top. His thick dark eyebrows were set in a mean scowl. He pointed in a couple different directions and thumped the back of his fist onto one of the men's chest. They began down the stairs and out of sight.

Megan's heart raced as she and Jack backed away from the window. She turned to him and said, "Now what?"

Jack took a deep breath and exhaled quickly. "They're looking for us."

"Do you know them?" she asked being hit with the fact that Jack was still, by blood anyway, one of them.

"Yeah, I do. The little guy's probably leading the search. He's been with the family for a long time. His father and my father grew up together." Jack went to pack their bags. "We're going to have to be really careful. They obviously don't know we're here, but if they ask around, we're in trouble. The kids who had this room saw me, the store clerk and a few shoppers saw me...we have to get out of here now."

"But what if they see us?" she asked walking between him and the bag he was in the process of packing. "We could just stay here for awhile or at least until they leave."

"No, that would be worse. Housekeeping is going to start soon. The people who I got this room from only had it for one night."

"Housekeeping," she said and smiled.

"What about it?" He continued packing.

"That's how we'll get out." He stopped.

"You lost me," he said shaking his head slightly.

"When housekeeping shows up, somehow we'll get a uniform. I'll put it on and as I push the cart, you can hide along side of it."

"It might work," he said not quite sure how but willing to try anything.

"How do we get a uniform?" she asked.

"Let's wait until we see a housekeeper, and we'll wing it. We have money so we can pay her off, or we can just steal the cart, or..." he said thinking.

"Jack, I'm not going to let you hurt an innocent person to save our sorry asses," she said thinking the worst.

"Not hurt," he said. "I wouldn't do that." She wasn't so sure she believed him.

They waited and watched from a space where the curtains

didn't meet. Watched as the sun was born. Watched as people stirred and began to make their way through town.

Just then they heard the squeaking of wheels come around the corner. The housekeeper was next door, but they couldn't see the person.

"Get into the bathroom," he said.

"What are you going to do?" she demanded. She was afraid for the unsuspecting stranger.

"I'm going with you," he said confusing her.

"The door will be propped open is my guess. Whatever we do, it'll have to be away from anyone who can see in."

"What are we going to do?"

"I don't know yet. Just trust me." The door from the room next to them closed, and he grabbed their backpacks and led Megan into the bathroom. He pointed to the bathtub. She stepped in, and he closed the curtain. She had to trust him. She didn't have a choice. He stood behind the bathroom door. There were sounds of rustling - changing the beds, trash bags being emptied, her mind raced. As the woman walked toward the bathroom, Megan started sniffling. Then the curtain of the shower squeaked a little.

The housekeeper cautiously looked around the door. Megan peeked from the curtain.

"Please ma'am. I'm sorry I scared you. I thought you were my husband," she sniffed and wiped her eyes with her bandaged hand. The housekeeper's look softened a little. Megan pulled the curtain open farther and let the woman see her in full - the scratches, the bruises, again the bandaged hand.

"Did your husband hurt you?" the woman asked with concern. She was dressed in jeans and a light coat over the maid's apron, which hung from the bottom of the coat. The only other clue that she worked for the motel was a name badge, her name was Myra. Megan nodded and started crying again.

"My friend," pointing to Jack behind the door, "he saved my life." Megan stuck her bandaged hand forward and said, "My husband cut me with broken glass. Jack lives next door, and he heard me screaming so he came over. My husband attacked him, too." Myra's attention turned to Jack. She saw the cuts and bruises on his face. "My husband was here looking for us. We saw him in the hall this morning," she said with her lip quivering.

"He was?" Myra's expression grew worried, and Megan nodded. "You poor thing. No wonder you're hiding."

"Would you please help us get out of here?" she pleaded and put her hand on the woman's arm. Jack stared. Her story was brilliant and believable.

"How?" Myra asked sounding as if she'd help but only to a certain extent. Myra was in her late forties, and it appeared life had been rough on her. She was of average build and had brown hair that just brushed her shoulders. Megan was sure she had been very pretty, but time and who knows what else, had etched themselves on her face. Megan imagined Myra was the kind of woman who probably had a lot of potential when she was growing up. A few bad choices or bad circumstances and she was working as a maid in a run-down motel in the cheapest area on the mountain. Megan was afraid she had caught a glimpse of her future. Not that being a maid was the worst thing in life, but not many little girls dream about cleaning 20 bathrooms every day and making other people's beds.

"Ma'am, if you'll let us hide behind your cart while you wheel it to the back stairwell, I think I can get her to safety," Jack said. Megan watched him as he worked on this woman. She was afraid Myra was smart and wouldn't trust him. Still, upon first look, any woman would want to believe him and want to be saved by him. He had a way of making you feel comfortable and uncomfortable at the same time. He could make you feel like you were the most important person in the room by the way he looked at you and talked to you. Megan remembered the night she met him. The smooth, rich tone when he spoke and Cary Grant eyes struck her as too good to be true. It had all been an act, just as this was. She was his target, and he used his skills to manipulate her - just like he was doing to Myra. She used the hurt to her advantage and let the tears form.

"My husband will kill me if he finds me. He even brought two of his friends with him to help hunt me. I just need a chance to get away... Please?" she begged. "Please help us get away." Myra nodded.

"Okay, honey. If that's all you need, I'll do it," she said with conviction. Megan burst with a sigh of relief and a smile in between deep breaths.

"Thank you," Megan said with sincere appreciation. Jack didn't speak. "There is just one little thing," she added. Jack's look warned her to stop her before she pushed too far. "If my husband asks you if you've seen us, please tell him you haven't, okay?" Jack looked relieved.

"Of course. What does he look like?"

"He's about 5'3, dark curly hair with dark eye brows. He usually wears a long black leather coat. I think he's with two of his friends."

"Oh, and he has a heavy New York accent," Jack added knowing Megan wouldn't know this information.

"He won't hurt you. It's me he's after. I can't do anything right when it comes to him."

They quickly worked out the details of how they would sneak out. Myra asked, "Do you have a car?" Jack and Megan looked at each other.

"No, we don't. It broke down," he said.

"How are you going to get away?" Myra asked.

"I don't know yet," he said. "Maybe go into the woods and walk?"

"There's a ski shop about a half mile down the road. The delivery truck stops there on its way down the mountain. My ex-husband drives it. He's probably there now so let's get you out of here."

"Thank you! You just saved our lives," Megan said as she hugged Myra.

Chapter Thirteen

After sneaking along side the housekeeping cart, a quick trip down a freight elevator in the back of the hotel and blocking themselves from view by ducking behind dumpsters, cars and even a park bench, Megan and Jack found their way behind a small, slightly run-down strip mall. There was a plain white truck sitting behind one of the shops with the back doors open. The truck wasn't as big as a semi - it was the size of one of those moving trucks that people rent. There would be ample room for them if the back wasn't full of ski equipment. Myra hadn't said whether or not her ex-husband would help them, so they decided to sneak onto the truck.

A man in a red plaid flannel shirt, jeans, a John Deere baseball hat and a navy down vest came out of the building and picked up a large brown box. He took it into the back of the building, and the door slammed behind him. Holding Megan's right hand, Jack began the approach to the back of the truck. He helped her climb up the back bumper and then used his left arm to hoist himself in as well. The truck was only half full. He quickly worked to arrange the boxes so it wouldn't be noticeable that anyone had maneuvered their way toward the cab. Jack and Megan crouched in the corner as the door to the store opened and a man's voice called, "See you next week, Rick." They took another look at each other as one of the doors closed. They lost light. Megan noticed for the first time how tight Jack held her as the other door slammed.

It was cold and dark. She shivered as Jack released her. He pulled the flashlight out of his backpack, so that he could see the boxes. He put the flashlight in his mouth, felt around in the dim light and opened a box. He stumbled over another box and opened it. He took the flashlight out of his mouth. "I found some coats," said quietly. He pulled the box back toward the corner with him.

"Jack, what are you doing?"

"Trying to keep us from freezing to death," he replied. He shuffled his feet so he wouldn't step on her. He made it back to her and knelt down handing her the flashlight. "Move so I can put some of these on the floor for you." She scooted to the side while he placed a layer of coats on the floor. He reached back in the box and grabbed some more coats. "Come on." He crawled onto the coats, and she followed. He took the flashlight from her. He leaned in the corner and took her arm as she tried to position herself on the coats. He pulled her to him, and she didn't resist. He spread the coats on top of her first, then himself. She snuggled into him and rested her head on his chest. He turned off the light.

"What happens next?' she said.

"I don't know. I guess we just take it one step at a time," he said. "You were amazing in the hotel." She smiled.

"Thanks. I can be a manipulative little bitch, can't I?" Although she had smiled at his praise, she wasn't at all sure she should be proud of her ability to lie to get what she wanted. While sometimes she seemed like a totally different person than Kristine Larkin, Megan was still Kristine at the core. When push came to shove, the ugly parts she didn't like and even some of the parts she did like, came to the surface. Megan wasn't sure if that was a good or bad thing.

"I don't think I would have called it that," he said. "I call it survival. I call it doing what you have to do to protect yourself."

"Is that how you justify doing it? I mean, you manipulated me, but it wasn't for your survival."

"No, it was for yours."

"Why didn't you just keep following me? You did it for a

month without me knowing. Why did you reveal yourself on the mountain?"

"It was too hard to follow you and not be seen. Especially after the plane ride - you'd recognize me," he said. "And I guess I was a little curious," he added.

"Curious? About what?"

"I had been keeping an eye on you for weeks. It's weird reading someone's file and practically becoming part of their life without ever talking to them."

"Hm," she said.

"What was that for?"

"I guess I just thought that was part of your job - remain a mystery or something," she said. He didn't answer her.

She hugged him tighter for warmth. The motion of the truck over the roads and the humming of the engine lulled her to sleep.

Chapter Fourteen

The motion of the truck and the engine coming to a stop woke her. She looked up and tried to see Jack's face through the dark. "Jack, what are we going to do?" she asked starting to feel trapped.

"Shh. We'll think of something. We always do." Just as the words left his mouth the doors to the truck jostled.

"What if they found us?" she asked breathing hard. One door swung open and light blinded them. They heard the sound of bags being put onto the floor, and then the door closed again. Both of them let out a deep breath of relief.

"Do you smell that?" she asked.

"Yeah. Smells like food," he said. "Stay here."

"Where are you going?" she wanted to know as she reached to try to stop him.

"I'm going to check it out," he said already standing.

"Be careful. He could open the door again. Or it could be a trap," she said.

"Great, I hadn't thought of that," he mumbled sarcastically.

After a few moments of boxes sliding, a beam of light bounced off the ceiling of the truck. "What is it?" she asked when she saw the light coming at her.

"Food. Myra must have called him to tell him we would be on the truck," he said as he sat down next to her on the coats. Except for the occasional zipper, the coats made for comfortable padding.

"Thank, God," she breathed as she sat up and took the bags from him. He propped the flashlight up against the coats. He took one of the bags, and they each opened the one they were holding. "Two bottles of water. What do you have?"

"Cheeseburgers and french fries," he said digging into the

bag. "There's a note in here," he said as he reached in, pulled it out and unfolded it. Megan reached for the flashlight and held it so they could see the writing. It wasn't very clear, but it was legible.

"Myra said you was hitching a ride. We're about two hours from the city. I'll need gas in an hour. Check on you then. Big Lou"

"He's helping us!" she said quietly excited. She reached out with one arm and hugged Jack around the neck. Realizing she had just nearly attacked Jack out of happiness, she quickly looked down at the food. Her mood turned from excitement to extreme caution, but she wasn't sure why. "I'm starving."

He took the flashlight from where she dropped it and placed it back up onto the coats. "We'll leave it on while we eat, and then turn it off to save the batteries," he said. She nodded without looking up. They sat with the bags between them.

"This may be the best cheeseburger and fries I've ever had," she said with a half-full mouth - something only a starving Megan would do.

"No wonder, you didn't eat your sandwich last night and we left without eating this morning," he said. They finished the burgers and turned off the flashlight. She didn't crawl back to him. She sat back against the truck wall.

The only instance in her life when time had passed slower was while she lie in a pool of blood on the floor behind a bar. She counted the number of pot holes the truck hit. Then she tried to remember the words to her favorite song, then her favorite movie. The silence was screaming in her ears, and she couldn't hear herself think. She sighed hard.

"Are you okay over there?" Jack's warm voice cut through

the cold air. Her sanity returned at the sound of his voice.

"Yeah, I'm just bored," she said nonchalantly and cracked her knuckles.

"Okay, we can do something to keep busy." She heard him rustling.

"What did you have in mind?" A hint of seduction in her voice she hadn't intended. She could tell from the silence he noticed it, too. She quickly became disgusted at herself - running for her life, and she's flirting. She cleared her throat.

"Mmm. How about good old fashioned conversation? Kind of like 20 questions," he answered.

"Fine, just what I had in mind," she said convincingly as she sat up.

"Me first," she said. "Have you ever been in love?"

"Wow, I didn't expect that. 'How do you live with yourself?' - maybe, but not that one."

"You didn't answer the question."

"Once," he said quietly. "And you?"

"It's not your turn yet," she insisted. "What was she like?"

"I'm not sure this is how the game is played," he said.

"Well, I have the rules right here, and it says it is," she insisted.

"Well, she was... She was normal. Actually, she was pretty incredible." He paused. She decided she was jealous.

"How did you meet?"

"In Jr. High we hated each other," he said with a laugh. "When we got to high school, everything changed. My junior year I was playing baseball. I was running off the field and looked up into the stands. There she was. She was smiling and clapping. She looked like...like an angel. Anyway, shortly after we started dating she found out she had leukemia. I pushed her wheel chair up to the stage so she could get her diploma when we graduated. Two weeks later, she died. It all happened so fast - it didn't seem real. I was so mad for awhile. That's another reason I decided to be a doctor."

"I'm sorry," Megan said - her voice soft and sad.

"Thanks. It was a long time ago," he said. There was a long silence. "What about you?" he finally asked.

"What about me?" she was still thinking about the young girl who died. She hoped he wouldn't lie about something so tragic.

"Have you been in love?" He reminded her of the original question.

"Oh jeesh," she sighed. "I don't know - maybe."

"There are no maybes - you either are or you aren't."

"Then I don't know," she said.

"Then you haven't been in love," he said. "You definitely know when you're in love."

"How?"

"It's not something I can explain, and it might be different for everyone," he said.

"Oh. Well, I guess I've cared for someone before. Maybe I could have fallen in love, but we didn't get the chance," she said.

"The editor?" he asked. She instantly became annoyed and a little apprehensive at the thought of him knowing so much about her.

"Well, this is a stupid game when you seemingly already know everything about me," she said crumbling a bag.

"Sorry. I'll shut up and let you talk."

"What's the point? Why don't you tell me about me," she said.

"What I read in a file isn't exactly a window into an individual's soul," he said. "There's plenty I don't know about you." She sat quietly for a minute deciding whether to continue being mad or get over it.

175

"Yes. Will," she said. "He had just told me how he felt when all of this stuff started getting out of hand."

"Will's the first guy you could have had feelings for? Didn't you date in high school or college?"

"Well, yes, but you probably already know that," she said uncomfortably. "I had a lot of guy friends and some guys I dated, but I was pretty focused on my dreams. I wasn't going to be one of those girls who gave up everything for a guy."

"And you don't think the newspaper guy would have wanted you to quit eventually?" he asked. She had never thought about Will asking her to quit. She always pictured them working side-by-side - having it all. Fantasies always had happy endings.

"I don't know," she said. "And I'll probably never find out."

"It's pretty impressive getting a job at a big city paper fresh out of a smaller college."

"Yes. It is. He told me when he hired me he didn't know what to expect from me. He said when he first read my application, he thought I was audacious. I don't even know how my application made it to his desk. I think he set up the first interview to humor the kid who thought the paper would be lucky to have her. I know I wasn't supposed to make it through the first round. The group of potential new hires was on a tour of the newsroom, and he was walking down the hall on his way to a meeting. I remember him stopping dead in his tracks. I had done my homework - I knew who he was. I smiled at him and then ignored him. I knew what I was doing. He came up to the group and introduced himself. He asked everyone who we were. An Editor-in-Chief wouldn't do that with a group of potential new hires. I think I knew right then and there I had the job."

"So what happened?" Jack asked.

"Nothing. He's professional, and I wasn't about to ruin my chances of being taken seriously by openly flirting or sleeping with the boss. Plus, he was married. We built a mutual respect for each other. I learned from him. When he took me in to protect me while I researched the story, he told me how he felt. That was as far as we got."

"You weren't in love with him?"

"I had never let myself feel that way. I think I've probably fallen in love with what could have been. You get pretty lonely when you lose everything. I've spent countless nights fantasizing about this perfect relationship with the perfect man. You and I both know it would never have turned out like that. Fairy tales are just that," she said.

"Is it his tie clip you keep with you?" he asked cautiously. She was startled.

"How do you know about that!?" she demanded.

"I've seen you hold it. On the plane, the night in the bar, in the cabin when you were drinking and I was working on your hand," he said. "You pull it out when you don't think anyone is looking or when you're anxious." She couldn't remember if she had been holding it or not, but she knew it was always with her.

"Yes. It's his." She touched her leg and could feel the tie clip in her jean pocket. "I miss him or maybe I just miss someone caring about me. Who knows?"

"Well, this is fun," he said facetiously. She heard irritation in his voice and thought she should soften her statement.

"I miss a lot of people. My friend Derrick - he's so funny and really smart. You'd like him. He wanted to be a doctor, too. Of course, there's my family. Hell, I even miss Burt Newman!"

"Who's Burt Newman?"

"Just some guy at the paper who used to drive me crazy.

He sat across from me. I always thought he was gross then," she paused before she said Will's name again. "Then someone told me why he was the way he was. He was taking care of his wife." She paused again wondering what happened to Burt Newman and his wife. "I guess things aren't always as clear cut as they may seem."

"This conversation keeps getting more and more light-hearted," he said.

"We just need to change the subject," she said. "Do you like sports?"

"Yeah, do you?" he asked.

"Yes. I played a lot of tennis in high school and college."

"I'm a Yankees fan," he said.

"Oh God," she said laughing.

"Hey, the Yankees have won more World Series titles than any other team," he said defensively.

"Of course they have. They can afford the best," she said. "That doesn't exactly make it fair for smaller market teams."

"Okay, so sports isn't a good topic for us either," he said laughing.

"Maybe not," she said laughing with him. "So we can't talk about love or sports. Obviously, politics and religion are off-limits. Have any other ideas?"

"What's your favorite song?"

"I don't have one," she replied.

"Come on. Everyone has a favorite song."

"You'll laugh."

"I promise."

"Oh. Okay. It's *Sway* by Dean Martin," she confessed reluctantly. "I used to go to my grandparents' house when my parents went out for date night. My grandpa would put on his records and then ask my grandma to dance. I'd just sit there watching them and think how lucky they were. Then, he'd ask me to dance, and I'd feel like the most special kid in the world." The thoughts should have brought back happy memories, but they just made her sad. Life was so simple then.

"That's very cool," he said quietly.

"Thanks. And yours?"

"Probably *Paint it Black* by the Stones."

"That's a good one," she answered. There was silence again. "Now what?"

"Well, you seem to have a pretty broad array of interests," he said. "I'm sure we can think of something that will spark a conversation."

"You sound surprised," she said. "Why?" she said defensively. "You need to be really well-versed when you're schmoozing with a source. I'm not stupid. I may have batted my eyes to get my job, but I was damned good at it and earned the right to keep it."

"Whoa, I didn't say...," he tried to speak.

"Well, that's the way most of your stupid city treated me when I moved there," she said remembering how rough the adjustment to New York had been for her.

"Megan, you don't have to be defensive with me," he said. She sighed.

"Shows how much you know about me. I'm defensive with everyone. I'm sorry. I've just always felt like I have to prove myself - like I'm not worthy unless I can one-up someone." She paused. "Damn it," she said loudly hugging her knees to her chest. "I have issues. I need so much therapy I could single handedly buy a shrink a three bedroom townhouse in Manhattan!"

"You know, I've spent some pretty stressful times with you. I've seen how quickly you react, how strong and courageous you are. At this point, I feel like I know you better than you know yourself," he said in a convincing tone. She

179

didn't know what to say, but she was glad there were no lights on in the truck. She bit her bottom lip and wondered if he could possibly know her as well as he thought.

The truck started to slow. After a few stops and turns, it rolled to a stop and the engine fell as silent as the conversation had.

"Stay back here. I'll check it out," he said and clicked on the flashlight. She didn't like the fact he could see her, but she couldn't see him when he shined it at her.

"I'm going with you," she said as she stood. "And get that thing out of my face."

"Why can't you just stay back here like I asked? Why do you always do the opposite of everything I say?" he asked.

"Well, if you must know, you can blame this one on nature. I have to go to the bathroom," she said knowing full well even if she didn't have to use the restroom, she wouldn't have listened to him. "Apparently you don't know me, or my bladder, as well as you may think." She grabbed the flashlight from him and started toward the doors. She turned toward him just in time to see him drop his head and shake it from side to side.

The door swung open and the light hurt her eyes. She squinted and hopped out of the truck. Myra's ex-husband was a large man. He was well over six feet tall and had a beer belly that made him look like he was carrying sextuplets. It was the kind of belly that made it impossible to tell whether he was wearing a belt. Funny how six-pack abs and a six pack of beer seemed at such opposite ends of the spectrum for Big Lou.

"Hey, I'm Big Lou. Did you get the food and note I put back there for you?" Lou asked. His green John Deere ball cap covered graying brown hair. It appeared he had made an attempt to tuck in his red flannel shirt, which gapped at the stomach to reveal a white under shirt - probably thermal underwear.

"Yes. I'm Megan. Thank you so much! We were starving," Megan said with a flirtatious smile as she touched Big Lou's big flannel arm. "I can't thank you enough for helping us out," she said sincerely. Then her look took a somber turn. "I don't know how much Myra told you, but my husband is a horrible person. He's hurt me very badly," she held up her hand and rolled her bottom lip into the slightest pout. She sized up Big Lou and tried to imagine Myra married to him.

"I just don't understand men," Big Lou said. "I'd like to meet the man who could hit a pretty little thing like you." Megan managed a weak smile at Big Lou and gently squeezed his arm.

"I'm sorry I didn't introduce you to my friend," Megan turned to see Jack standing behind her looking at her with a sarcastic grin on his face. "This is Jack."

"Nice to meet you," the men said at the same time and exchanged hand shakes. She thought she saw Jack put extra strength into his - probably intimidated by Big Lou's stature, she thought.

She glanced around. They were at a gas station. "I'll be..." she said pointing toward the back of the station, and Jack nodded. Lou tipped his hat, and she could feel one or more sets of eyes on her as she walked toward the back of the station. The door wasn't locked. She opened it and went in. The restroom looked as though it hadn't seen a scrub brush in years, but it was good enough. She did her best not to touch anything more than she had to and used her foot to flush the toilet. She also used a paper towel to work the handle on the hot water tap, which could only manage lukewarm. She looked into the dirty mirror, sighed and shook her head. She must have aged five years in the last two days. She used the paper towel to open the door and began to walk out.

Someone grabbed her from behind. Trying to struggle, her legs left the concrete walk, and her arms were pinned to her sides. She couldn't get free, and she couldn't scream through the hand over her mouth. Just then the short man from outside the hotel room appeared before her. Her panic grew, and her eyes widened. She kicked her legs harder. Her ribs hurt from the pressure of him squeezing her.

"Look, we're not going to hurt you," the man said. "I'm Agent Roberto Massoni from the FBI." Her mind soared from one thing to the next, and she stopped her struggle against the man holding her. She knew her eyes still showed fear, though. "If we let you go, promise you won't scream? We need to talk to you about the man you're traveling with, Jack Rawlings. You're in a lot of danger, ma'am. Can we let you go?" She nodded once. The man let her go, and she looked back at him to see what he looked like.

"I want to see your ID," she said. The man opened his coat and pulled a leather billfold-type holder. She took it from him and opened it. On one side was an FBI badge, the other a photo ID. She studied it and then the man's face. It was him in the picture. "How did you find us?"

"The cell phone one of you took off our man has GPS tracking." She mentally scolded herself for being so stupid. "Look, we have to talk fast. Mr. Rawlings is a dirty agent who works for his father. We think you're in grave danger." Grave danger, she thought. She had never heard anyone actually talk like that. "We need to know where he's taking you. We're trying to get more information to put him and the rest of his family in prison," he said.

"I don't believe you," she said thinking something didn't seem right. "He could have already killed me. He's had a lot of opportunities."

"He knows we're following him. Now, ma'am, I'm sure you didn't know what you were doing, but you've helped him kill several of our men. We even have reason to believe you may have single-handedly killed some." She swallowed hard and couldn't speak. The shot she had fired into the woods rang in her ears. This was too much for her. "Look, we're not holding you responsible. We want him."

"We're going back to his family's house," she said without thinking about it first. The man looked at the other two men and nodded.

"Makes sense. He's probably going to prove his loyalty by taking you there. Get back on the truck with him. Do what you're doing," he said.

"Wait, I need to..." she began as she heard Jack's voice from the side of the building.

"Megan? Are you okay?" The voice got closer. The man put his finger to his lips and disappeared into the woman's room with the other man in black. She cleared her throat.

"Yeah, I'm fine," she said. Her voice shook when she spoke, and she walked toward him. They nearly ran into each other rounding the corner.

"Hey, sorry," he said laughing. She didn't look up and stiffened at his hands on her arms.

"Just watch where you're going," she said and forced a stiff laugh before rushing past him. She went into the gas station and paced the motor oil aisle. Big Lou came in to pay. She walked up to him and glanced at the clerk. "Um, hi. Did Jack give you some money for that?"

"Yes, ma'am. He did. He's a nice guy. Seems to care an awful lot about what happens to you," he looked her up and down but not in the obvious way some men did.

"I know you've done an awful lot for us already. Could I ask you to do me one more, please?" She used her best damsel in distress eyes, and it wasn't much of a stretch for her at this point.

"If I can," he said. She reached into her pocket and pulled out some money. She took the gas receipt and the pen on the counter to write down the number for Will's cell phone, his name, her name and a quick message. She said a brief prayer that the number was still his and she remembered it correctly.

"As soon as you drop us off, please call this number and read this note. The man's name is Will - he's my boss. Whatever you do, please don't tell my friend I gave this to you." She glanced over the man's shoulder and saw Jack by the truck looking at her. She formed a smile and said, "He's so protective - he gets a little jealous if anyone else helps me. Will you do this for me, please? It could be a matter of life and death." And she picked up a pack of gum and paid for it. She glanced out the window at Jack.

"Uh, sure," he said.

"I think we better get going," she added. As she walked out of the station she looked around, but there was no trace of the men she had talked to moments earlier.

She got to the truck and hesitated before letting Jack help her up the step. Her heart was beating so hard she thought it might jump out of her chest. They made their way up to their mound of coats as the door shut. Now what? She thought to herself. She dropped to her uninjured hand and knees, grabbed some coats and hugged them to her as she sat with her back against the wall.

"You okay?" Jack asked.

"Mm hm," she said quietly.

"Want to talk some more?" he probed.

"No, I'm tired," she said. She put her head against the wall and closed her eyes. She wanted to run through every event.

The only thing she knew for sure was that she wasn't sure of anything.

Chapter Fifteen

Megan pretended to sleep for the duration of the ride ignoring Jack's whispers of her name. Yet she was aware of every noise he made. She played back the moments since she had gotten on the plane and first noticed him. She ran through every word, every gesture that was made and was no closer to understanding anything. She used to trust her instincts. She used to know how to read people.

When the truck stopped and they were standing in a rest area somewhere outside of New York City, she searched Big Lou's face with hopeful eyes. Did he remember the receipt? Did he remember her plea? If he did, would Will still have the same cell phone number? Would he believe some strange man with an unbelievable story? She swallowed hard to free her throat from the growing lump and felt tears well in her eyes. Now, what? Her mind raced. Damn! She had had an entire truck ride to plan her next move and all she could think about was Jack. Her heart beat erratically and sweat formed on her forehead and upper lip.

"Megan?" Jack said taking her arm. "You okay?" Think quick, she thought.

"No," she gasped. "Can you get me something to drink, please?"

"Lou, Will you stay with her for a second?" Jack asked as he took off for the rest area building. Megan waited for him to be out of ear shot. She looked up at Lou.

"Do you still have the note?" He nodded worried. "Good. The phone number is for an old boss of mine who is probably the only one who can help us get away from my husband. Jack doesn't know him and might be hurt if I ask anyone else for help. He thinks there might be something more than friendship between us, but there isn't. Know what I mean?"

"Sure," Lou said. "You just leave it to Big Lou." Jack was jogging back toward them.

"Thank you so much. You've been so wonderful to me," she said. Jack tapped the top of a soda can.

"This is all they had," he said and popped the top. He handed the can to her, and she took a sip. "Drink it slow." He looked up at Lou and added, "We haven't been able to eat very well. I'm sure she's just tired or maybe the hand's infected."

"Are you sure you want me to drop you here?" he asked.

"Yes, we'll be fine," Jack assured him. Megan looked at the tab of the can. She wasn't so sure. However, she was fairly certain she had convinced her new friend to place the call for her, and for that she felt better.

She was still armed with a gun and a cell phone with GPS tracking. She would have to be even more careful.

As the truck pulled out of site, with their bags slung on their backs, Megan looked up at Jack. "Now what?"

"We're not that far away now."

"Why didn't we stay with him?"

"He was going in the opposite direction. We would have ended up farther away."

"Remind me again why we're going to your family's house. Isn't that a bit like pouring lighter fluid on the hot coals you're walking on?" She wasn't sure she should change the plan since the gas station FBI agents, and potentially Will, thought that's where they were headed.

"I don't know any other way out of this for us. I don't think anyone would expect us to go there. If we can get something - anything - to help us then I think it's worth a shot."

"Like what, Jack? After dear old dad slaughters some poor, unsuspecting guy or worse - his wife - does he confess it in his Hello Kitty diary? You know, kind of like: 'Dear Diary, Today I had two eggs for breakfast, bought a new tie and arranged for some poor bastard to get shot in the head?' Or how about a row of video's by the TV? 'Uncle Ed's Wedding,' 'Ralston's Pre-School Graduation,' 'Our Hit Men's Greatest Hits Volume 1?'" she said sarcastically in a near panic.

"I don't know," he said quietly. "Probably nothing quite that obvious. Maybe you're right. Maybe we should pull some agents into it. Only problem is you don't know which ones you can trust and which ones you can't."

"Tell me about it," she snorted under her breath - her mind racing. She wondered why he would say that if he wasn't a "good" guy. Hell, maybe he said it because he isn't a good guy. Crap, she thought. Now her head hurt. Any way she looked at it, a change in plans may do her more harm than good. "Screw it. I say we go. I want to march up to the front door, ring the bell and beat the hell out of whoever opens it," she said with a laugh that sounded mixed with dementia. "I'll even dress up like a Girl Scout selling cookies. I'll say, 'one box or two' and then POW! I'll poke their eyes out with my merit badges." Jack just looked at her while she ranted. She stopped, took a deep breath and said, "My head hurts."

"Uh," Jack said tentatively. "Why don't we talk about the details of how we get into the house later." He looked at her with a cautious stare. "There's a rental car place about 15 minutes away. Let's get a car, and then we can figure it out," he said and tried to take her by the arm.

Chapter Sixteen

"I thought you said this place was only 15 minutes away," she said suspiciously as she took a big step over a fallen tree. Jack had wanted to stay out of site from the cars on the highway. This raised her suspicions, so she kept a hand in her coat pocket that carried the gun. She also made sure he was always in front of her, and the roar of a passing truck could be heard on the highway about 50 yards on her left.

"Give me a break, okay? I've never walked it before, and I don't need a time Nazi nagging me the entire time," he said losing his patience more rapidly than usual.

"Go to hell," she said with meaning. "When we get to this god-forsaken car rental place - if it exists - why don't you go your way and I'll go mine? If I disappear on my own, I'll probably do a better job of protecting myself than the morons who have claimed to try so far."

"Because we'll both be dead in a matter of weeks," he said talking to her as though she was stupid.

"Sounds like it might be a couple more weeks than what I'll live if I follow you," she said sarcastically.

"Look," he said turning and slamming his bag down. "What the hell has gotten into you? You go to the bathroom, and all of the sudden I start getting more attitude than the usual," he said. She could see him trying to calm down and regain his composure. He started more calmly, "I can only protect you if I know where you are."

"Protect me?! You're a joke! Do you know how many times I could have been killed in the last couple of days?" she yelled and threw her bag at him.

"I've never tried to hurt you," he yelled back.

"Yeah," she grunted. "This is how normal people spend

vacations. Van crashes, flying off snowmobiles," she said as she ticked them off one by one on her fingers. "I've been shot at and… and… you made me ice skate," the last part sounded funny even to her.

"Ice skate?" he said with a raised eyebrow and a laugh pulling at lips.

"It's not funny," she fought to remain serious.

"Well, if you want to go there then you tried to hurt me, too," he said.

"What? I did not."

"You made me stand in the cold banging at a deadbolt while you were inside the cabin," he said.

"That's stupid," she replied.

"That counts," he said staring at her triumphantly as though he had just won some sort of contest. She was speechless. Her lips twitched.

"I hate you," she grunted as she picked up her bag.

"I know," he said as he picked up his bag.

"Go," she said wanting to keep him in front of her.

Another 20 minutes passed before they came to the exit. There was a small but national rental agency, some gas stations, a half empty strip mall, a motel, a K-Mart and several fast food restaurants.

"Let's get something to eat," he said as they walked through the parking lot of the strip mall. "Maybe it will improve your disposition."

"Bite me."

"Nice. Anything sound good?"

"Whatever you want is fine with me."

"Fine. Let's go."

"Great. Kind of like the last supper," she mumbled. She was too tired to sleep and too hungry to eat. They ended up in a truck-stop style diner that advertised home cooking.

There was very little conversation. Jack ate well. Megan managed to eat some food and picked at the rest.

"Jack?"

"Hm?" he said with a mouth full of fried chicken strip.

"Why should I trust you?" she said without looking up. There was a silence. She couldn't tell if he was thinking or finishing chewing.

"If I were you, I wouldn't trust anyone - you shouldn't." It wasn't what she expected to hear. "Why do you ask?"

"I don't know," she hesitated and decided not to tell him. "How long do you think it will be before we're there?"

"Well, we have to rent the car and then it's about an hour and a half from here," he said.

"Sure about the hour and a half part?" she asked remembering her 15 minute walk that turned out to be closer to 45 minutes to an hour.

"Yes. I'm sure. That's drive time," he said without any sarcasm.

"Excuse me," she said. "I'll be back." He nodded while she scooted out of the booth. She walked toward the restrooms. She had been careful to make sure she took the side of the booth facing the restrooms. She looked for a pay phone and found one situated between the two entry doors. Quickly, she glanced over her shoulder to make sure Jack wasn't watching her. She dialed and said some silent prayers hoping there was someone somewhere listening to them.

* * * * *

"Are you sure you're okay? You're sweating." Jack said when she finally returned to the booth. He sounded genuinely concerned. She noticed he had eaten some of the food off her plate.

"Fine," she lied through a forced smile. She felt terrible. The check was on the table face down. "Are you ready to do this?"

"Sure," he said and picked up the check as he made his way out of the booth. He paid cash at the register, and they made the short walk to the rental agency.

"You may need to do that thing you do if it's a guy clerk," Jack said as they neared the door of the building.

"What thing?"

"The pouting lip, big eyes, damsel in distress thing you pulled with the housekeeper and truck driver," he said.

"I don't know what you're talking about," she said adamantly but knowing full well what he wanted her to do.

"Whatever. Just do it, because the ID I'm going to give him doesn't look a thing like me," he said.

"Maybe you'll get lucky and it will be a woman. You can do that thing you do," she said sounding nasty and accusatory. He grabbed her by the arm and pulled her to the side of the building.

"What the hell has gotten into you?" he asked.

"Get off of me," she growled and jerked her arm away from him. He looked at her with a hurt and tired expression. "I just want this to be over - one way or the other," she said.

"You and me both," he agreed. "You just seem... well... meaner," he said. She drew a deep breath.

"Sorry," she said, but there was no sincerity to it.

"Let's just try to manage to co-exist for the next couple of hours. Can you manage that?" he said.

"I'll try."

"Fine," he said and opened the door for her as they reached the entrance to the agency.

"Can I help you?" a middle-aged gentleman said from behind the counter. It had to be Burt Newman's long-lost twin brother, she thought. While they didn't look the same, they had the same taste in clothing and hair styles. Flirting with a Burt Newman clone wasn't going to be easy for her.

"Hi," Jack said. "We'd like to rent a car, please." The man started pounding on the keyboard in front of him. Poor keys.

"What size?" the man asked.

"Full-size," Jack replied. He looked at Megan and said, "I like to be comfortable." She rolled her eyes, which the clerk saw and seemed to enjoy. She smiled at him and winked. "That's it," she caught Jack mumble almost inaudibly.

"Can we have a red car?" Megan asked very sweetly.

"What difference does it make? A car's a car," Jack said looking at her as though she'd asked for a ride on the space shuttle.

"Red's my lucky color," she said as though she had been mortally wounded by Jack's comments and looked at the clerk with a pleading expression. Jack looked at the clerk as if to say it's not a big deal. "I always wear something red. Always." She gave the clerk as sly smile and bit her lower lip. Megan wasn't wearing any visible red which caused the clerks eyes to grow wide as they roamed over her. Flirting was easier when the target was this eager. She glanced at Jack. She remembered him doing their laundry and realized he knew she wasn't wearing anything red.

"Let me check, but I think we've got a red one out there, ma'am," he scratched his dandruff drenched scalp as he stabbed at the keys with his pudgy little fingers.

"Thanks. It really means a lot to me," she said with an innocent smile. Jack took her by the arm and walked a step away from the counter.

"All this and you're worried about the color of the damned car?" She pulled her arm away again and stepped back to the counter. When it was time, Jack handed the man behind the counter a credit card and driver's license - neither of them his. The man didn't even look at them before swiping the card and punching in the license information and handing them back to Jack.

As they walked toward the cars Jack thought out loud, "You know...the van we were in was red."

"Is it the van's fault it was driven off the side of a mountain? Besides, we survived that, didn't we?" she said nonchalantly.

The ride was quiet, and Megan fidgeted with Will's tie clip.

Chapter Seventeen

The house was isolated. It sat way off the road on acres of land and had a solid, brick fence around it with black, wrought iron gates that met at the driveway. Trees provided extra privacy. The house itself was a two story, white, colonial place. It had four tall, white columns running up the porch to the roof. Jack drove slowly past the house and looked at it carefully. He continued on and wound around so that the car was behind the house on another, minimally traveled road. Heavy trees and the wall-like fence separated them from the monstrous back yard. Jack pulled off the side of the road. He looked at her. She was staring at the tie clip.

"Okay. We're losing light, which may work to my advantage. I want you to take the car and go somewhere safe. Whatever you do, don't go to the police - I don't know who's on his payroll. Half the force is driving cars my family gave them."

"Then what?" she said thinking, planning.

"Do you still have the cell phone?"

"How do you know I have a cell phone?"

"Not much gets past me, Babe," he said turned toward her with one arm resting on the top of the steering wheel.

"I threw it in the garbage at the restaurant," she admitted while looking at the little piece of gold in her hand. He nodded.

"You go, and I'll find you somehow to let you know when everything's done," he said checking the rear view mirror. She took a deep breath to keep the car from spinning around her. "If you don't hear from me within 12 hours…"

"Oh, God! Jack, I have to tell you something," she felt sick to her stomach. Despite the heat from the car, she was still freezing.

"What?"

"Remember those guys from the hotel?"

"Yeah?"

"I talked to them. They grabbed me at the gas station. They said they were the FBI and you were the bad guy and everything they said made sense. Actually, nothing made sense. I was so confused."

"Just tell me what happened," he said. She could tell he was trying to avoid a conversation about her inner turmoil.

"They had badges - I saw them. They asked me where we were going, and I told them. But something didn't seem right and now I know what." Her breathing had become heavy. Jack ran his fingers through his short, graying hair.

"What?" he asked.

"The badge. The type on the guy's name didn't match the rest of it - it was close but not exact. I know because of my background in journalism and type facing. Jack, I thought - shit, I don't know what I thought. But you can't go in now. They know," she said reaching out her bandaged hand and putting it on his arm.

"No, I'm tired of this. Somebody's got to put a stop to this and it might as well be me. If I can't stop them, I'm going to die trying," he said in a low tone.

"Jack, there's more," she said slowly.

"More?" He looked at the hand on his arm.

"I made some phone calls when I said I went to the bathroom. In minutes a news crew in a helicopter will be flying overhead. That's why we needed a red car - so they knew what to look for when they got here. I figured if everyone knew I was here then you...they couldn't hurt me. I also had Big Lou call Will, and I left him a voicemail. He knows where we are, too. I told him to call someone he trusted in the FBI," she said.   He sat quietly taking this in and processing it.

"No, this could be good." He shifted in his seat to face her more. "You're sweating."   He put his hand on her forehead. "You have fever. Your hand is infected. I'm going in. Wait for the news crew and when they get here, have them take you to a hospital."

"You can't go in," she said.

"I have to, Megan. Neither of us is ever going to be free again unless somebody does something to stop them. I have to do this for you, my mother and for me," he took his right hand and put it on her left cheek. He moved his thumb back and forth over the feverish, chapped skin. He stared into her eyes until she closed them. "Remember, you need a doctor. If they don't show up, you get out of here. At the first sign of trouble drive as fast as you can and don't ever look back, okay?" he said solemnly. She opened her eyes, and as she did a tear fell. "Hey, we're going to be okay," he smiled. She nodded and wiped her face. Before she knew what was happening, he pulled her face to his and kissed her.   Their lips were so chapped they were cracked, but that didn't stop either of them. He abruptly pulled away and said, "See, ya."   And he was crossing the street and heading down a slope full of trees toward the wall before she could speak.

She watched until he disappeared and decided to sit behind the wheel of the car just in case. She opened her door and walked around to the driver's side. As she began to open the door she caught a flash of a reflection in the window. Before she could turn around, a hand knocked the door closed and away from her. She thought to scream, but the hand was over her mouth before she could. She tried to reach for her coat pocket for the gun but another hand beat her to it. She heard a voice say, "Come on. Let's go."

Chapter Eighteen

Megan was shoved into the back seat of a black sedan. She felt pain in her left hand. Once she righted herself, she saw the back of a man's head - the driver - and then glanced to her left and saw the man sitting next to her. One of the men was the guy who grabbed her at the gas station.

"Where are we going?" she demanded. No answer. "Who are you?" Again, no response. Both men stared straight ahead. The car raced into the driveway of the house and through the open gate. Megan turned in her seat to see the gate close behind them. She looked down at the bandage on her hand. It was bleeding again. She glanced up at the man next to her. As much as it hurt, she squeezed her hand to produce more blood, adjusted the bandage and then put it on the black leather seat next to her. If anything was going to happen to her, she wanted her blood to be in as many places as possible. The car screeched to a halt on the side of the house, and she flew forward. She ran her hand along the back of the front seat and bent to touch the carpeting in the car. "Nice stop! Been watching too many cop shows lately? Let me give you a little tip - you're the bad guys, and you end up dead or in jail. Didn't Batman tell you crime doesn't pay?"

The doors flew open, and the man next to her grabbed her by her left arm. She put her bleeding hand on the arm of his black suit coat. He pulled her out of the car and nearly dragged her through the side door. "I can walk!" she yelped, and he let go as soon as the door closed behind them. One man walked in front of her, the other behind as they passed down a long hall. She let her left hand casually brush up against the wall whenever she could. She reached her left hand out and tapped the man in front of her, "Hey! Where are we going?" She demanded again knowing it was futile but wanting to get traces of her blood on him as well. She had quietly "died" on the floor of a bar. This time, she wasn't going down without a fight, she thought. No matter how scared she was, she was never going to show it. She wouldn't give them the satisfaction.

They rounded the corner and walked through a living room area. She touched everything she could without drawing too much attention to herself - tables, a chair, a door frame. They walked into an office area. Behind the desk stood the man she had talked to outside the bathroom.

"We meet again, Ms. Larkin. Welcome. Mr. Rawlings will join you shortly," he said with a grin.

"And short is something you'd know about," she said confidently and flashed her best "I know something you don't" smile. "Mind if I sit down? I'm exhausted. Plus, that will put us more on eye level," she said and sat in one of the two wing-backed chairs in front of the desk. She rested her hand on the arm of the chair. The man behind the desk grinned with amusement.

"You are a feisty little bitch, aren't you?" he said smiling as if they were in a contest to see who could be the most over confident. "It's a shame about your upcoming fatal accident. But then, you can't kill a dead woman," he said with mock pity in his voice. She was jelly inside, but managed the strongest front she could.

"That will be all for now, Maestro," a man's voice said as it came through a door on the left side of the room. Maestro moved away from behind the desk and stood to the side. Megan knew instantly Robert Rawlings had come into the room - she remembered his face from the photos. He was in black dress pants and a blue dress shirt. His gray hair was streaked with black and slicked back revealing a bit of a widow's peak. He had Jack's eyes but without the kindness. She wondered how she could have missed the likenesses. He looked more like a handsome politician than a ruthless murderer. If he had looked as dangerous as he was, she would have melted through the chair and into the floor. Instead, she mustered her courage.

"Hey, RJ. Good to see you," she said. "What's with the Maestro thing? Is it because maestros stand on boxes when they conduct?" Robert Rawlings laughed out loud.

"That's very funny," he said. "Maestro conducts business for me, hence the name."

"Whatever," she said sounding disappointed it wasn't something more creative or demeaning. She spotted a candy dish on the desk. "Mind if I?" she asked, leaned forward and took a piece while wiping her hand on the edge of the mahogany desk. "I have a real sweet tooth."

"Help yourself," he said and nodded to the dish. "I understand you've become quite friendly with my son."

"Ralston's in jail. I have no intention of getting friendly with that animal. He's a murderer, you know," she said pretending not to know what he meant. "I don't know if I'd be proud of him if I were you."

"You're good at this game," Rawlings said amused. "You know very well I'm talking about my other son, Jack."

"Jack's your son?!" she said faking surprise. "No kidding? Huh! Who would have known? Would you have guessed that?" she asked Maestro. He didn't answer. She shrugged. "So, let me get this straight. Your own son hates you enough to want you in prison?" She made a disapproving face that reminded her of Will's secretary. "You must really suck at being a father. I wonder how he turned out so well with you as a dad. Must have been raised by someone else." She popped a piece of candy in her mouth and chewed through her closed mouth smile. Rawlings was staring at her. She fought the panic back, so it wouldn't show on her face.

"You're making this very easy for me," he said.

"I can be very helpful," she said. "What am I doing?"

"See, in a few minutes I'm going to place a call to the police and report two intruders in my home. When they get here, they'll find two bodies shot dead - yours and my dear, long lost son Jack's," he said confidently and dramatically. "I'll be heartbroken, of course." She swallowed hard but managed to speak.

"Wow. That does sound tragic. I bet you had some practice when you murdered your wife," she said playfully but began to worry about Jack. "You'll be able to tell your story to the news crew I've called. You might want to do something about your skin - I don't know how the yellow will look on camera with the lights. Of course, I already told them my side of the story. You know - how you've been hunting me because I know what a filthy bastard you are, yada, yada, yada... Shhh... I'll bet if you listen closely, you can hear the chopper overhead." The room was quiet for a second. There it was - distant but there. She breathed a sigh of relief inside. "See? I can be very helpful," she continued. "Oh, and I'm really sorry about the mess I've made," she said as she raised her hand from the chair to reveal a blood spot. Mr. Rawlings looked down and saw the dark spot. His face remained stoic. "I've left quite a trail of blood since this goon over here made my hand start bleeding again." She turned in her chair and spoke directly to the man standing behind her, "You are not a nice man. Does your mother know how you treat women?" Quick glances back and forth between the men let her know she was saying the right things. "I'm sure you wanted the house to look nice on TV, but what could I do?"

"Well, it seems you're more prepared than I anticipated,"

he said looking down at the desk briefly and shuffling some papers.

"You underestimated me, didn't you?" she asked with mock disappointment nodding her head.

"It appears so," he said sounding more confident than she thought he should.

"Hey, it happens to the best of them. Now, here's the way I see it. If Jack and I don't walk out of this house unharmed, a news crew is going to release the story that we disappeared here because our very red rental car is out on the street behind the house. I'm sure there are at least one or two straight cops or FBI agents who have been itching for an excuse to shoot your ass, so I'm sure you won't have time to find all of the blood spots. You certainly won't have time to get them all cleaned by the time this place is swarmed. I'm very thorough," she added nearly in a sing-song voice. "I've even left a detailed message of the weekend's events on some important people's voice mails as a little insurance," she talked slow and confidently now.

The man shook his head slowly. "So you're pretty sure you won this battle."

"No. No. I'm pretty sure I just won the war. See, if you manage to stay out of jail this time and anything happens to us, you'll have a lot of explaining to do. Given our history, I don't think you want that." He looked at the men standing behind her.

"Take her upstairs until I figure out what to do," he said gruffly. "And make sure she doesn't leave any more blood stains, you idiots." The two men stepped forward from where they were standing behind her. One grabbed her arms and began duct taping her wrists together. Rawlings turned to Maestro, "Start cleaning house," he said. Maestro nodded and disappeared.

"Ouch! You know, you're just giving me more to tell the authorities," she said watching her wrists.

Before she knew it, she was on her feet and being led back through the living room and up a grand staircase, down a hall and into a very pink bedroom. She heard RJ Rawlings call from downstairs. The men threw her into the room without binding her feet, locked the door and left her. Apparently, Rawlings and his goons were more concerned about what police would find downstairs than guarding her. She looked around. It was bright and floral from the wallpaper to the bed. She tried to rub her hand on the pastel flowers on the comforter, but it was harder now that her palms faced each other. She went to open a few dresser drawers. They were empty - must be a spare room, she thought. She went to the French doors and opened one. It led to a large balcony and an alarm sounded. What did she care? She had to get out.

She walked quickly along the side of the house looking in windows and doors. She found Jack. He was in another room, duct taped at the wrists, ankles and mouth. He was obviously struggling to get free, on his side on a bed. She tried to open the French doors, but they were locked. He looked up startled and somewhat relieved. The sound of the helicopter grew louder. Megan looked around, but there wasn't anything on the balcony she could throw through the glass. The flower pots were large and filled with dirt. She stepped back and kicked where the doors met and almost fell backwards. While her legs were strong from all those nights of running, the last several days had made her weaker. She took a deep breath and mustered all the strength she had. She kicked the doors again. She did it again. "Come on," she screamed at herself as much as at the doors. It took her several tries, but she finally managed to kick the wooden door open.

She rushed in and pulled the tape off Jack's mouth and

began working on the tape at his wrists. Once unbound, he worked on his ankles and then turned his attention to the tape around her wrists.

"How did you get here?" he asked. He picked at the tape with what little fingernail he had then bit at it.

"Long story," she said. "Hurry up. That's our ride," she said.

"But I didn't find anything yet," he insisted. He got the end of the tape lifted and unwrapped her wrists.

"Jack, let's get the hell out of here," she pulled him in the direction of the door. He came out on the balcony with her and rushed to the ledge with her right behind him. He looked over.

"I'll go first. Once I'm on the ground, you climb over, and I'll catch you," he said as he swung a leg over the wall and touched the ledge on the other side. He held on with both arms as he swung the other leg over. He tried to use the traction from his snow boots to cling to the brick support column and inch his way down. Finally, he let go and fell on the thin layer of snow covering the concrete porch below. He jumped to his feet and yelled, "Come on."

She swung her leg over the wall but wasn't tall enough to touch the ledge. She scooted to her right and tried to grip the concrete she sat on as she began to pull her other leg over. She had her feet on the ledge when she heard voices shouting in the house. "Jack! Catch me!" She let go, and he used his body to break her fall. They scrambled to their feet.

"Go! Go!" he yelled, and they began running through the backyard to the clearing just beyond the pool where the helicopter could land.

There were four men in dark suits standing on the balcony with weapons drawn. No one could hear the orders "Let them go!" being shouted from the door on the porch below because of the whipping blades as they descended. Gun shots accompanied the pounding noise, and the air swirled.

Jack kept Megan in front of him, and she reached her hand behind her. He took it and they were within 15 yards of the copter when Jack let go. Megan stopped and turned with horror on her face.

"NO!" she screamed. She ran back. Jack had fallen face down. She squatted next to him and looked toward the house. The bullets had stopped and Mr. Rawlings was standing behind the pool. "Jack?" she yelled.

He looked up and managed the word, "Go!"

"Get up!" she screamed. "You're getting on this helicopter if I have to drag you!" She saw blood on the upper, right part of his back. He struggled to get to his feet. She used every bit of power she had to brace him and pull him to the copter. She fell in backwards and pulled Jack in on top of her. "GO!" she screamed.

She looked at the camera man who was still filming and then at the young blonde reporter, "Damn it, help me!" she screamed at her. The reporter, whose jaw hung open pulled herself together and dropped the microphone she was holding. Megan knew what she was doing when she called her old nemesis from her childhood, Tara. Tara Tierra would do anything for a story - she was just like Megan had been. Megan knew Tara didn't care whether she and Jack lived or died, but she also knew that this footage would give Tara national exposure and possibly seal a deal with a national television news organization.

Tara helped put Jack on the floor next to Megan. It was a tight squeeze, but Megan pulled herself up onto her side. "Jack! What should I do? Jack!"

"Pressure," he whispered.

"Pressure," she repeated. She grabbed Tara's scarf, balled it up and pulled Jack up enough to press it into the hole in his back. "Get us to a hospital! Now!" she screamed toward the pilot. "Hold on, Jack. Hold on," she said and used her other hand to hold his hand.

Chapter Nineteen

Megan opened her eyes slowly not even sure where she was or how she had gotten there. The last thing she remembered was landing on the roof top of a hospital in a news helicopter. She had watched as Jack was put on a stretcher and wheeled away. He had held onto her hand until he was pulled out of reach. Then she was put on a stretcher. She closed her eyes, and that was it.

She didn't know how long she'd been asleep or what had happened during that time. Her throat was sore. Everything hurt.

"Hey, you." She heard a familiar, deep voice with a slight southern drawl. She blinked and turned her head. Her eyes brought Will's face into focus. He was sitting next to her bed smiling at her. She smiled, and he leaned to her.

"Hi," she said groggily.

"You sure surprised the hell out of me," he put his large, soft and warm hand on the side of her face.

"What happened?" she asked. Her mouth was dry.

"You had to have surgery on your hand, and you have an infection," he said stroking her hair.

"What about Jack?" she asked. Will's eyes showed a flash of jealousy and then a smile.

"He's lucky to be alive. The doctors took the bullet out of his back, but he's still in serious condition," Will said soothingly.

"But he'll be okay?" she asked with concern in her voice.

"He'll be okay," he said. "I couldn't believe it when I got the message from some trucker that you were alive. I thought it was a joke. And then, when I heard your message..." he said with his voice trailing and emotion flooding his face. "You have no idea how happy and how afraid I was."

"I think I can guess how afraid you were," she said with a weak smile. He shook his head as if to admit what he said had sounded crazy. "Can I have some water?"

"Sure, Sweetheart," he said and reached for a plastic pitcher on the nightstand next to her bed. He poured some water into a small plastic cup, put a straw in it and held it for her to drink.

"Thanks. That's better. What happened to Rawlings?"

"From what you left on my voicemail and the footage they had of his men shooting at you and Jack as you ran away," he paused and swallowed hard. "Well, the Feds finally had probable cause to get a search warrant for the house and Rawlings' properties. There was also a lot of media and public pressure, which made it nearly impossible for any judge to deny one. Once they got inside, they found some incriminating stuff on some of the computers they confiscated. They had tried to clear the hard drives, but technicians recovered them. Rawlings is going to jail for a very, very long time. You're safe," he said smiling. She breathed a sigh of relief and tears filled her eyes. Emotion built and built.

"I'm free?" her voice cracked when she spoke.

"Yes, Sweetheart. You're free now," he stroked her cheek. "You should probably try to get some rest. I'll be right here when you wake up, and your parents are on their way back from getting dinner." Megan smiled at this news and nodded. She closed her eyes to sleep as Will kissed her forehead.

* * * * *

The following weeks brought countless interviews with Federal and local law enforcement agents. Megan had become Kristine again - even if in name only. She spent hours apologizing and explaining to friends and family what had happened the day of her "death" and giving them the highlights of her life over the last two years. Her parents stayed for several days, and were finally convinced it was okay to go home when her infection was under control. They wanted Kristine to move home with them, but all she could manage to say was, "We'll see." She didn't know what she wanted.

Most surprising was Burt Newman's daily visits. His wife had passed away and, as Will said, Burt thought pretty highly of Kristine. Burt's appearance and disposition toward people had improved now that he didn't have the demands of his ailing wife. He even seemed to enjoy the drama when his visits overlapped with Derrick's.

After Derrick's first visit, he returned with makeup and hair styling implements. He told Kristine that if she didn't feel good, he would at least make her look good. He repeated gossip he'd read in the tabloids at the grocery. He even brought his surgeon boyfriend to meet her. When Will wasn't with them, he'd ask about both Will and Jack. Kristine couldn't tell him what he wanted to know, which only frustrated Derrick. She did send him on fact-finding missions to check on Jack's condition. It was easier to ask Derrick than it was to ask Will. Derrick wasn't very popular with the nurses or doctors as he completely took over and offered suggestions on how best to care for his friend.

Then there was Will. Not only was he popular with the nurses, Will was sitting next to her hospital bed every time she woke - day or night. Somehow he always managed to be clean shaven with fresh clothes. Will could spend as many hours as he wanted to with her now that he and Emily had divorced. He said it was final about a year ago. He phoned the paper regularly and his daughters every evening before they went to bed.

While she enjoyed her visitors, it was somewhat overwhelming to her. She'd been alone - even when she was in an over-crowded classroom - for two years. Days passed slowly as she gained her strength and fought the multiple infections she had from her wounds. She was thankful for the medications that let her sleep, because her mind raced with questions about what came next in her life when she was awake. Finally, after a week and a half, she was well enough to get out of bed.

"Will?" Will looked up from the newspaper he was reading. "I really need to see Jack," she said. Will nodded, but he obviously wasn't thrilled with her request. He folded the newspaper, removed his reading glasses and put them both next to the phone on the nightstand.

"I'll get a wheelchair," he said and stood.

"No. I want to walk," she insisted. "I need to move my legs again. Can you help me?"

"Sure." Will helped her put on a robe, walk down the hall to the elevator and then to Jack's room. Jack had been moved from intensive care to a private room. She knew she had looked better - her hair was in a pony tail, and she didn't have on any makeup. Derrick hadn't been to see her yet that day to work his magic. Will supported her as she walked.

"This is it," he said when they reached Jack's door.

"I'll just be a minute," she said to let Will know she wanted to go into the room alone. Will nodded and leaned against the wall.

"Let me know if you need me."

"Thanks," she added with a smile and knocked on the door.

"Come in," she heard Jack say.

"Is it okay?" Kristine walked in slowly. She saw Tara Tierra sitting next to Jack's hospital bed and felt her jaw drop.

"Yeah," he said, and his smile widened when he saw it was

her. "It's great to see you, Megan."

"Uh, it's Kristine again," she interrupted. "Hi, Tara."

"Hi, Kristine," Tara said standing with bright white teeth screaming past her pink lipstick. "You look terrible, dear." Kristine inadvertently rolled her eyes. "Here. Take my chair. I was just leaving - have to get back to work." She turned to Jack and said, "I'll see you later." Her perfect hair, her perfect clothes and her perfect makeup and expensive perfume brushed past Kristine, and she was gone. Kristine was speechless. She suddenly wished Derrick had paid her a visit this morning to fix her up a bit. She used her right hand to smooth her ponytail. She was thankful for Tara, but she still disliked her - it was a habit too hard to break. She walked over and sat next to Jack's bed.

"So, Kristine it is. I like it," Jack said snapping her out of whatever zone she had entered.

"Uh, yeah. I didn't see a need to keep Megan, and the agents agreed with me. Being on the national news kind of puts an end to any protection program you may be in."

"Good. Kristine - I like it," he said again nervously. "So, how are you?"

"Not shot. How are you?" she said smiling. She noticed his arm in a sling that held it tight to his body.

"I'll be fine. I might need another surgery, but I'll be fine. The bullet didn't hit my spine so I'm really lucky," he said. "What about the hand?"

"I had surgery. Doctors said you did a great job on it, though. I may have a little nerve damage, but I can live with that. The infections took some time to react to the antibiotics, but I'm going home in a day or two," she said smiling. She looked down at her hand wrapped in bandages. She had some gauze taped to the worst cuts on her face. "I'm going to have some minor scarring on my face, so I may tryout for some haunted houses in October or something," she added nervously. "If I were more like Tara, I could have made it through everything without messing up my hair and makeup."

"Tara couldn't have done what you've done. The scars will only make you look more beautiful," he said. She couldn't help feeling grateful to him for his words.

"Did you see our story on the news and in the papers?"

"I've been kind of out of it," he said. "But a nurse saved the newspapers for me," he said smiling. "You were amazing, you know. You should be safe now. Rawlings is going to jail for a long time, and we got his top people."

"How do you feel about that? I mean, I know there has to be some relief, but he's still your father."

"No. My father is the man who raised me. I was lucky enough to have two mothers, but I only have one father. I may even change my last name."

"Change your name?"

"Yeah. I don't want anything to do with those people. I want to distance myself. At least you got your name and life back. You can live the life you wanted and not worry about what or who is lurking in the shadows."

"I hope so. I think we could both use a little happiness for awhile," she said. "So, what was Tara Butmacher doing here?"

"Butmacher?" Jack said laughing and wincing.

"Yeah, that's the princess' real name," she said in a tone that wasn't flattering. She suddenly decided she didn't want to know why she was there. "Um, listen Jack. I just wanted to say that I'm sorry for being such a...well...bitch and for not trusting you when I should have. I also wanted to say thank you for keeping me alive."

"I should thank you, too. If it wasn't for you, I wouldn't be alive. You saved my life in the woods and probably a couple times when we were at the mansion," he said sounding truly grateful. She laughed a little and was about to speak when she saw Jack's eyes dart to the door. She turned her head, and Will walked into the room. She was a little disappointed with the interruption.

"Are you okay, Krissy? I really should get you back to your room. You're not strong enough to be out of bed for long," Will said as he put his hand on her shoulder.

"Almost," she looked at Jack. "Jack, this is Will. Will, this is Jack." Will took his hand from her shoulder and shook Jack's available hand.

"I need to thank you for everything you did to help bring her back to me," Will said.

"It was my pleasure," Jack said quietly, a vein in his forehead noticeably throbbed.

"We better get going. The nurse is going to track you down and make you ride back to your room in a wheelchair," Will said looking at Kristine and putting his arm out to help her out of the chair.

"Yeah, okay," she said still looking at Jack. She smiled and stood with Will's help.

"Be happy, okay?" he said looking at her with such intensity her stomach leapt into her throat. She swallowed and nodded. Why did she feel like crying?

"You, too." She took a step toward the bed, reached out and took his hand. She leaned over and kissed his forehead. Without looking at him again, she let Will help her walk out of the room.

"Are you okay," Will asked once they were in the safety of the elevator. She nodded. Saying anything would reveal the lump in her throat. Will rubbed the small of her back while she stood in the elevator waiting for the number of her floor to light. She wanted to turn around and be held by him, but her body wouldn't move. He even had to give her a little nudge when the doors finally opened just so her feet would take a step forward.

* * * * *

She sat in the hospital bed and played with her Jello. She thought about how ironic it would be to have an eating disorder like anorexia and end up in the hospital. If anything could make you not want to eat, it was probably hospital food. Everyone who comes into the hospital got an IV, or so Derrick had once told her. Maybe they should give everyone a feeding tube, too, she thought. Will's voice broke her train of thought.

"Is it Jack?" he asked. She was startled by the sound of the voice and the question.

"Is what Jack?" she replied.

"This mood. You should be happy to be back with your friends and family. I was really hoping you'd be happy to be with me. Then a trip upstairs and you seem a million miles away." She pushed the food tray away.

"I'm sorry. I don't know what it is," she said. "I guess I'm just confused about what happens next."

"You get your life back," he said reassuringly.

"That's the problem, Will. I don't know who I am anymore," she said. "I want to be a reporter or a writer, but I don't think I have the drive I used to have. It's just weird, you know? So much has happened to me over the last two years. How do I just go back to being the old me?"

"This is probably more pressure than you want or need right now, but what about us? I still want a future with you," he said.

"I honestly don't know," she said. "The thought of being with you kept me going all that time I was alone. I care about you so much."

"I thought I heard a 'but' at the end of that sentence," he said. She sighed and shrunk down into the bed. "It's Jack, isn't it?"

"No," she said unconvincingly then changed her answer. "Maybe. I don't know."

"I understand," Will said.

"No. I don't think you can," she said growing sure of what she was saying. "We were literally running for our lives, and all we had was each other. Will, I went so long with just fantasies of what my life could be like with you knowing it would never happen. I had accepted that you weren't going to be part of my future. I sat in a virtually empty apartment for two years creating the perfect image of you and our perfect life together. Then I meet this man who drives me crazy. He's far from perfect, but we shared this really intense experience. He saved my life. I'm not stupid - I know he kept me in front of him while we were running to the helicopter."

"From what I saw, you saved him," Will replied.

"Before that."

"That's his job," Will said.

"It was more than that," she responded. "I feel some sort of... I don't know - bond with him." Will's eyes fell to the floor, and he remained quiet. "I'm sorry. I'm not saying I don't want to be with you. I'm just saying I think I need time to sort all of this out. I feel like I'm starting my life over again for the second time. I need to figure out who this Kristine is and what she wants before I can make any decisions about my future. I do have feelings for you, Will. I just feel like I need to rid my mind of the fantasy life I created before I can give you a fair chance. No one can live up to what I've created in my mind, and I don't think you want to start this relationship with no where to go but disappointment." She reached for his hand, and he gave it to her. "Be honest with yourself. Haven't you done the same thing? Please, Will. Can you just give me some time to sort out my life?" He stared at their hands and stroked her skin.

"You've changed, Krissy. You're more mature - less impetuous." He looked at her and smiled. "I waited for two years while I thought you were gone. I can wait some more," he said. She smiled. "And you may be right about starting fresh without expectations."

"Thank you. I don't know how long this is going to take, but I promise you I will let you know when I figure out what's going on in my head." Will nodded.

"I'll try not to pressure you," he said. "I take it you're going to want some time alone?"

"Not necessarily alone - I was alone for two years. I just may need some space," she said. "I'm also going to need support from the people who care about me, and honestly, I don't think I'm going to be able to do this without you in my corner. Is that okay?"

"You come to me for whatever you need," he said and stood up from the chair he had pulled next to her bed. He took his coat from the hook on the back of the door and walked back to her. "You know how to find me." He touched her shoulder and kissed her forehead then walked away. As he opened the door, he turned to her and smiled. "Remember, I love you." She smiled at him and wondered how he could love someone he didn't even know.

Chapter Twenty

Kristine was mid-sentence on the computer screen when her door bell rang. She hurried to finish her thought before she got up from the desk. The bell rang again.

"Who is it?" she called as she hit the save button. The answer made her stop in her tracks.

"Jack," said the voice on the other side of the door. Her mind jumped from reason to reason as to why Jack Rawlings was standing at the door of her condominium. She went to the door and opened it with a smile. The sight of him standing there made her forget her composure, and she hugged him. He was wearing a black t-shirt tucked into dark jeans. His face and arms were tan.

"Hi," she said as she pulled away. "How are you?"

"Fine," he said politely.

"How are you really?"

"Pretty good. My wounds are healed, but I'm still in physical therapy. They have me pushing papers for awhile at work - only part of it's because of my injuries, though."

"They're pretty mad at you for disobeying their orders when they took you off my case, huh?" she said as she backed through the door. "Come in." Jack stepped into the entry hall, and she shut the door. She walked past him, and he followed her into her condo.

"How's the hand?"

"Good," she said holding it up and turning to him. "Nasty scar, but I almost feel it's a badge of honor at this point." She stopped walking when they were in the living room and pulled her hair away from her forehead. Her hair was now streaked a balance of Kristine brown and Megan blonde. It was longer than Megan's, too. "I can cover the worst scar on my face with my hair." He stood there for a second looking at the scar, and then his eyes moved to her eyes for a moment before she looked away.

"It's a nice face," he said softly as he walked around her and looked over the condo. "Nice place. Must have cost a fortune," he said looking around.

"Thanks. I sold a book and the movie rights." She decided not to tell him about her anonymous donation to an organization that helps battered women start over or how she was going to do some work with them when she finished the book. "Oh, you'll probably get a release form from the lawyers. I'm writing it now on a pretty tight deadline, actually. The advance was pretty nice, and I get the byline - or whatever they call it when you're an author of a book," she said with a laugh. "It's hard to change the jargon."

"And what about a job after the book is finished? Will you go back to the paper?"

"I don't know yet. I most likely won't go back to the paper. Believe it or not, I may even teach again, but I haven't made any decisions yet."

"So, you're writing a book, and you had time to unpack?" he asked looking around again. She wondered if he was looking for something specific or if being an agent made him take in surroundings more than the average person.

"Funny - dead people don't have many belongings," she said and sat on one of the sofas in the living room. "There wasn't much I wanted from my old place. I bought some furniture, but most of the drawers and closets are empty." He sat down next to her.

"Starting over again, huh?" he said seeming to understand.

"Yeah - that's exactly what I'm doing. This time it isn't so bad, though. I have my friends and family around," she said. "Speaking of friends - how's Tara Butmacher?"

218

"Who? Oh! Tara Tierra," he said with a sly smile. She wasn't sure she wanted to hear the rest of what he had to say. "I have no idea. She hung out at the hospital almost daily for awhile, but then she probably decided she didn't like all those sick people. She left a voice mail on my phone a couple of times, but I keep forgetting to return her call. I guess she feels some sort of obligation to us since she rescued us."

"Yeah, that's why she visited me so often," she said sarcastically. "I don't think her motives were quite so heroic." He just looked confused for a moment then smiled as if he had been let in on some sort of secret. She suddenly felt like she had betrayed her best friend. "Can I get you something to eat or drink?"

"No. Thanks," he said. "So, speaking of friends and family - how's Will? Which one is he again - a friend or family? I don't see his and her coffee mugs or any other sign of him around here." She smiled.

"Will and I are still trying to figure out what we want," she said. "Of course he's been here, but he doesn't live here." She decided to change the subject before he could ask questions about Will she didn't want to answer. "By the way, why are you here? I haven't seen you in months - since that day in the hospital. I thought maybe you'd contact me when you got out. I'm sorry I didn't come to see you again, but it was... I don't know. I guess it was just hard to see you for some reason."

"I understand. Why am I here? That's a good question," he said. "I just wanted to see how you were doing and whether you're okay. And..." He stopped. "Uh... How are you doing? I mean, beside the physical scars. You've been through a lot."

"I'm doing well, or at least I am most of the time. I still have a lot of nightmares and some trouble sleeping," she said adding the last part for honesty's sake.

"You know," he said and stopped. She waited for a second for him to continue, but he didn't.

"Know what?"

"Oh, what the hell," he mumbled to himself. "You know, if I hadn't been in that hospital bed unable to move, I would have been sitting next to your bed when you woke up. I would hold you while you sleep, so you would never be afraid of anything again," he said without looking at her. Her heart sputtered for a moment. She wasn't sure if she was surprised more by his words or the fact he looked scared. Vehicles crashing, bullets flying, hit men trying to kill him and he was afraid of her.

"And what about Will?" she said somewhat playfully wondering if he had forgotten someone *was* there.

"I would have shot him," he said and then laughed. It wasn't a funny - ha ha laugh. It was a nervous laugh. She smiled at his nervousness. "Okay, I wouldn't have shot him, but this isn't a joke," he added.

"I'm sorry," she said. "I've just never seen you... well, intimidated. You're usually so smooth and know what to say." He sighed.

"I don't know if I've ever been in this situation," he replied. "I usually know what the hell I'm doing." She smiled again. "God knows I've tried, but I just can't stop thinking about you. Remember when you asked me why I revealed myself to you on the mountain?"

"Yes. You said it was because you couldn't stay as hidden."

"Well, that wasn't the main reason," he said. "I'm good at what I do. If I want to stay hidden, I stay hidden. I'd been watching you for a month, remember? I watched you go into the school or your apartment, and I wanted to know more. I wanted to hear the sound of your voice. I wanted to find out what went through your head when you got that far away look in your eyes."

"You did?" She thought she should be concerned in a stalker/victim kind of way, but oddly enough, she wasn't.

"Yes."

"I don't understand. I thought I was just some lost cause to you - someone you felt obligated to help. I practically threw myself at you that last night in my room when the power went out, and you didn't take me up on the offer."

"I couldn't. I couldn't make love to you based on all the lies. If I had stayed with you that night, you would have hated me for it. You never would have let me help you, and you most likely would have never wanted to see me again. As much as it killed me to turn my back on you that night, I had to consider the consequences if I didn't."

"Wow," she said taking in this new information. He had put a lot of thought into their encounters, and she hadn't realized it until now.

"I wanted to know more than what I had read in the file. I had to find out who you were."

"And?" He put his hand on her thigh.

"And I decided you can drive me crazier than anyone I've ever met, but I like it," he said with his eyes still fixed on the floor.

"Well, this definitely complicates things," she said standing and walking to the kitchen for a bottle of water. "Are you sure you don't want anything?" He was watching her now.

"Complicate things? How?" he asked and then followed her. She leaned against the counter and folded an arm over her pink shirt, which was tucked into her jeans.

"I didn't think you had these kinds of feelings for me. For all I knew, you were with Tara." She shivered at the thought. If she decided to be with Jack, she would have beaten Tara.

She knew Tara was hanging out in a hospital to land the hot guy with the gun - maybe even to take him away from her. Her new life wasn't about winning, though. It was about being happy. "I've just been trying to figure out how Will fits in my life. Now I have to decide what to do with you."

"Are you taking requests?" he said and stood very near her. He smelled good. "Did you decide whether you love the guy?" She took a deep breath and held it for a minute.

"I love Will in this old, comfortable kind of way. He's so kind and so…" she searched for the correct word.

"He's boring," Jack said. She felt the need to defend Will. Jack inched closer to her. Again, she wanted to move, but she couldn't.

"Not boring," she insisted.

"Normal?" he tried again.

"Yes. He's kind of like gym shoes - you're just comfortable in them, and there's no excitement - like guns and dead bodies. You put on your gym shoes, and you know you're going to the gym and the grocery store." Jack laughed. "Wait, I'm not saying that's a bad thing. I've had enough excitement to last a couple of lifetimes." Jack didn't find that too funny.

"What am I?" he asked.

"You're like a new pair of black pumps with straps around the ankles," she said.

"I'm not sure I know what that means - I've never worn black pumps before," he said with a grin. "Thank God."

"You're sexy and dangerous and you know that you're going to feel amazing for the first few minutes. You put on the black pumps, and you don't know what kind of a ride you're in for. Then all of the sudden your feet start to hurt, and you don't know if wild is what you want anymore. Does any of this make sense?"

"I'm almost afraid to admit it does," he nodded as he spoke. "So... Now what?"

"Now I try to figure out if I'm the Kristine who wants to be comfortable or the Kristine who wants to roll the dice. Or, maybe I'm the Kristine who wants it all. I just don't know. Quite honestly, I'm still figuring out who I am now."

"You should have it all," he said as he inched closer to her again. His body was touching hers now. He moved the hair away from her ear and neck and whispered, "You should have the gym shoes, the pumps and hell, some loafers or whatever they call other shoes." She couldn't help it - she leaned into him as they both laughed.

"Are you taking your name out of the hat then?" she asked looking up into his chocolate eyes. He stepped back so their bodies were no longer touching.

"No," he said. "I'm telling you not to settle if it's not one of us. I'm not going away, though. Maybe you get the pumps and find out they're sexy and comfortable as hell if you just break them in a little." She smiled and nodded as she tried to process things in her head. He moved the hair off her forehead, gently brushed the scar with his finger and kissed it.

This new life wasn't going to be as simple as she had thought...

www.ingramcontent.com/pod-product-compliance
Lightning Source LLC
Chambersburg PA
CBHW020834260626
47169CB00003B/980